The Hen Night Prophecies:

Unlucky in Love

Jessica Fox

little
black
dress

First published in Great Britain in 2010
by LITTLE BLACK DRESS
An imprint of HEADLINE PUBLISHING GROUP

A LITTLE BLACK DRESS paperback

1

Cataloguing in Publication Data is available from the British Library

ISBN 978 0 7553 4960 9

Typeset in Transit511BT by Avon DataSet Ltd,
Bidford-on-Avon, Warwickshire

Printed and bound in Great Britain by
Clays Ltd, St Ives plc

HEADLINE PUBLISHING GROUP
An Hachette UK Company
338 Euston Road
London NW1 3BH

www.littleblackdressbooks.com
www.headline.co.uk
www.hachette.co.uk

little black dress
· IT'S A GIRL THING ·

Dear Little Black Dress Reader,

Thanks for picking up this Little Black Dress book, one of the great new titles from our series of fun, page-turning romance novels. Lucky you — you're about to have a fantastic romantic read that we know you won't be able to put down!

Why don't you make your Little Black Dress experience even better by logging on to

www.littleblackdressbooks.com

where you can:

- ♥ Enter our **monthly competitions** to win **gorgeous** prizes
- ♥ Get **hot-off-the-press** news about our latest titles
- ♥ Read **exclusive** preview chapters both from your **favourite** authors and from brilliant new writing talent
- ♥ Buy **up-and-coming** books online
- ♥ Sign up for an essential slice of romance via our **fortnightly email** newsletter

We love nothing more than to curl up and indulge in an addictive romance, and so we're delighted to welcome you into the Little Black Dress club!

With love from,

The *little black dress* team

Five interesting things about Jessica Fox:

1. I can't resist stopping to look at newly married couples emerging from churches.

2. My palm-reader told me I have a lifeline that is shorter than my heart line. I assume this means I will be with my husband Rob in this life and the next. I just hope he will have learned to pick up his socks by then.

3. I have a phobia of elevators. On our honeymoon, the Eiffel Tower was definitely worth it. Until I realised I'd left my camera at the top.

4. I was once on a hen night where the groom appeared in the early hours and started chatting me up!

5. If my house was on fire, and I could only rescue one thing, it would be my antique tarot cards. Sorry, Rob.

By Jessica Fox

The Hen Night Prophecies: The One That Got Away
The Hen Night Prophecies: Eastern Promise
The Hen Night Prophecies: Hard to Get

To my wonderful parents –
thank you for believing in me.

Libby Forster could hardly believe her luck. The Jasmine Hotel was so amazing she could have pinched herself. But bruised arms were not a good look when you were wearing a strappy green maxi-dress and glittery sandals.

Libby tucked her long golden hair behind her ears and stepped from the lush green gardens into the bar. Although it was night time, the air was warm and soupy so Libby was pleased to spot her colleagues sitting out on the terrace where it was cooler.

Tom was standing at the bar chatting to a man who Libby recognised as one of the production team from the *The Indian Prince and I*, the big-budget movie that was the reason they were all here in gorgeous Thailand. Tom caught her eye and smiled warmly. Wow, that man could make her stomach flip like an acrobat! Even though they had been seeing each other for a couple of months, he still had the same effect on her as the first time they kissed. His hawk-like profile and strong forearms were showcased tonight by a streamlined white T-shirt and he looked great.

He didn't beckon her over. But that was fair enough, Libby thought, as she decided against her usual cider and ordered a cocktail. Tom was here to network and promote the company, not to hang out with her. And he was always most insistent that, when on business time, they kept things strictly professional. Libby was more than happy to go along with this because she was still the newest junior casting agent at Cast Away and she didn't think that sleeping with the boss was the way to win friends and influence people.

'Hey, Libby!' Her fellow agent and friend Kyle called out, waving at her across the bar. 'We're over here. Come and join us.'

Ripping her gaze away from Tom, Libby waved back and wove her way through the busy bar towards them. Her heart sank a little when she saw that Hilary was part of the group, wearing her usual expression of someone sucking an acid drop, but she felt a bit more cheered by the presence of Kyle's girlfriend Janine. Like Libby, Janine was a junior casting agent and they shared the same dry sense of humour. But looks-wise the two girls were polar opposites: Janine being a petite and curvaceous brunette while Libby was a tall, slender blonde. Relationship-wise their lives were in total contrast too: while Libby dated a string of fun but totally unreliable men (she was hoping Tom would be the exception to this rule) Janine had been with Kyle for years and was five months pregnant. 'How's it going, hon?' Libby asked, slipping into the seat beside Janine.

'Oh, I'm coping,' she said, shifting uncomfortably. 'Have you managed to get a glimpse of *him* yet?'

Him, was Dash Suri, Bollywood legend and total sex god. Libby had nearly combusted with excitement when Tom had let slip that Dash was the leading man in the film. She had had a huge crush on him when she was a teenager and, although she was now a mature and sensible twenty-four, rather than a star-struck fifteen, Libby still felt rather faint that her idol was in such close proximity.

'Not yet,' she said, 'and I have no idea how I'll manage when I do. He's so— Janine, are you all right?' Her friend's eyes were filling.

'Kyle's being a total bastard,' she replied, a tear trickling down her face. 'He's hardly spoken to me. I'm sure it's because he thinks I'm fat and ugly. He's probably got someone else on the go.'

Libby glanced across at Kyle who was deep in conversation with some of the cast members. Naturally gregarious, Kyle was always the life and soul of the party, radiating charm and wide-boy confidence wherever he went. He was also desperately ambitious and never missed an opportunity to meet potential new clients.

'He's just talking shop, babes,' Libby reassured her, giving her friend's hand a squeeze. 'He adores you. And besides, you're not fat, you're a BOGOF. Two for the price of one, which makes you even more gorgeous!'

'Well, I didn't realise *this* was in the bargain. I wish he could puke his guts up and waddle round like a heifer for a while,' sniffed Janine.

Libby patted her arm sympathetically as her friend went on to list Kyle's failings: so far tonight he'd commented on Hilary's high heels when he knew she couldn't wear them, had thoughtlessly ordered champagne when he knew she couldn't drink, and now he was ignoring her. It was all paranoid nonsense – Libby knew Kyle loved Janine and was over the moon about the baby – but trying to convince Janine of this was harder than splitting the atom. In the end she just listened patiently, while trying her hardest to stop her thoughts from drifting back to Tom.

Now and again their eyes would meet and his gaze would slip over her body as though he was already peeling off the maxi-dress to reveal the skimpy bronze bikini beneath. Libby felt herself grow so hot and flustered that she had to look away.

Honestly, she thought wryly, Janine doesn't know how lucky she is! At least her partner acknowledges they're together. It was fun having a secret relationship with her sexy boss but recently Libby had found herself wondering what life would be like if they were a proper couple. Surely it wouldn't matter that much? People met at work all the time and coped with being professional. It wasn't as though she and Tom would spend all day having passionate sex on the boardroom table!

Unfortunately.

No. It was time they came clean. Her relationship with Tom was two months old now and it was getting to the stage where she was having to lie to her colleagues and her sister about what was going on. Things were going to have to change.

'What's the matter? Have I said something to upset you?' Janine was asking, concern written all over her pretty, freckled face. 'You looked really sad for a minute there.'

Libby ripped her thoughts away from Tom and pasted a smile on to her face.

'I'm fine. Just thinking about things,' she hedged.

'About your mystery man, you mean? It's OK, I'm not going to ask you to spill the chilli beans,' Janine promised, holding up her hands. 'I know how secret you like to keep your love life.'

'I'd tell you if I could. In fact, I'd love to tell you, but it's complicated.'

Janine's hands flew to her mouth. 'Oh, my God! You're seeing a married man!'

'I am not!' This was one rumour that Libby had to nip in the bud before it flowered. 'Honestly, I'm not.'

Janine looked doubtful. 'Whatever you say. Anyway, I thought you said you were staying well away from men after what that psychic told you at your sister's hen night?'

Janine laughed but Libby groaned. She had tried her best to forget.

'What was it she said?' Janine went on, but Libby couldn't bring herself to repeat it. 'That's it: you are a danger to many men!'

2

'Don't worry, she could have got it wrong,' Janine said, once she saw the panicked look on Libby's face.

'Angela's never wrong,' replied Libby with a sigh, wishing she could say that the fortune-teller was a charlatan. 'She was spot on with everything.'

Janine's brow pleated. 'Maybe I should ask her what's going on with Kyle these days.'

Libby opened her mouth to point out that this hardly required the skills of a psychic: Kyle was clearly stressing about the forthcoming promotion which had been internally advertised. Getting that job, he'd told Libby as they'd queued for their luggage, would just about cover the shortfall when Janine went on maternity leave. But, remembering that Kyle had sworn her to secrecy, she shut her mouth. What was it with having to keep secrets lately?

'I think I'll go and see her when we get home,' Janine was thinking aloud now, 'and maybe I'll get my runes read, too. You never know, it might help.'

Libby nodded. This was another thing they had in common. Like Janine, she adored all things spiritual and was often to be found with her nose buried in *Fate and Fortune* magazine, or consulting online tarot spreads. When Janine had given Libby the card for Angela Lambert, the tarot reader she swore by, Libby hadn't hesitated to book her for Zoe's hen night.

Janine continued. 'If she tells you something then it'll come true. She was spot on about the baby.'

'She knew all about me, that was for certain,' Libby agreed. 'I'd better be really careful. My horoscope in *Heat* this week says I need to look before I leap.'

The two girls looked at each other, wide eyed.

'That man of yours had better watch out!' breathed Janine.

Libby bit her lip. This morning she'd checked her stars online, in the papers and in the five gossip magazines she'd brought with her and she was still none the wiser. Should she stay in or go out? Would she meet a stranger or should she focus on her partner? Were abundant finances winging their way to her or should she listen to Russell Grant and save? Argh! It was all so confusing. If only somebody would come along and tell her exactly what to do.

She sighed. Hiring a fortune-teller for Zoe's hen night was such a good idea at the time. Zoe had been adamant no strippers would be tolerated and had even vetoed a night out clubbing, opting instead for a quiet night in with a select group of friends. A hen night should be a wild occasion, in Libby's opinion, a chance to let down your hair and party! But Libby would never want to upset Zoe, so a psychic had seemed like the perfect solution. They'd sink a few bottles of white wine, have their cards read and then giggle about the predictions of tall dark strangers, career changes and bouncing babies.

What could possibly go wrong?

It had been a good plan, Libby told herself firmly; it wasn't her fault things hadn't quite worked out as expected. For a start, the fortune-teller had turned up looking more like someone's nan than a travelling gypsy – all M&S slacks and curly grey perm rather than tasselled skirts and hooped earrings – and her prophecies had been rather odd, too. There were none of the usual generic platitudes, and several of the girls had been rather ashen faced after their individual readings. Zoe had been especially quiet and had refused to discuss what she'd been told, insisting instead that they all concentrated on the nibbles and wine. Only the antics of zany Fern Moss, who flamenco'd a drunken dance with a tray of flaming Sambucas held above her head, had brought a smile back to Zoe's pale complexion.

Sitting in the hotel bar on this balmy September evening Libby recalled her own reading with Angela. She'd had it done so many times that she hardly needed to be told to shuffle the tarot cards, before cutting them into three piles.

Angela picked up a selection and laid them out on her red tablecloth in the Celtic Cross formation. For a moment she studied them, before shaking her grey head.

'You have a taste for adventure, lovie, don't you?' she asked. 'You crave excitement and risks.'

'Mmm,' Libby had mumbled. This was all true but seeing as she was dressed in Billabong, Quiksilver and Roxy gear it could have just been a lucky guess. Libby was a believer, not a sucker.

'But no matter how fast you run or how many times you choose to risk your neck, you can never escape one person: you,' the psychic continued. Looking up, she fixed Libby with a beady stare. 'You need to accept yourself, my love. You're different from your sister but equally as valid and cherished. The High Priestess is in the ascendancy of your spread, which means you have the potential to be a very strong woman indeed.'

'Cool,' said Libby. 'Girl Power!' Then, because Tom had just asked her out, she added, 'What about the men in my future?'

'Let's ask the cards, shall we? Turn the top one over on the left-hand pile.'

Libby did as she was told and flipped one over, her heart plummeting when she saw the blank eyes and sharp scythe of the Grim Reaper.

'Oh my God, am I going to die?'

Angela laughed. 'We're all born to die, my sweetheart, but this card isn't talking about physical death so don't look so worried.'

'Phew.' Libby giggled nervously, although her heart was still break-dancing somewhere in her chest cavity. 'I was wondering if I ought to cancel my trip to Snowdonia next weekend.'

She'd cancelled it anyway, just in case.

'This card is no laughing matter,' said Angela gently. 'It's a warning, my love and a very serious one. You can't ignore it!' Her bright eyes searched Libby's as though looking for the answer. 'Sweetheart, *you* are the danger! You are a danger to many men. Take special care in September because that is when I see this all happening.'

Libby gaped at her. 'Are you sure you haven't got things the wrong way round? Most of the guys I meet are a danger to me!'

Take Tom for instance; deadly attractive, but her boss. Surely that didn't bode well?

But Angela had slumped in her seat. Suddenly she

looked exhausted, as though dredging up this warning had drained the life from her.

'I'm sorry, lovie, I can't tell you any more. I can only pass on what the cards show or what my guides tell me. It might not make sense now but it will become clear in the end. And remember September. Please take the greatest of care in September.'

Well, it's September now, Libby thought as she sipped her cocktail. *Maybe I'll be a danger to men by breaking their hearts?* Then she laughed aloud. She'd hardly break Tom's heart. If she was totally honest with herself she knew he only picked her up when he had nothing else on. Generally, this suited Libby; no-strings sex with a handsome older man left her free to climb and canoe and party. Although it would be nice if they could stop skulking around – all the secrecy was starting to get her down. Libby knew that Janine was already suspicious. Just lately she was always asking where she was off to whenever she left the office.

'What are you two whispering about?' Hilary demanded as, uninvited, she joined them. An empty glass in one hand, a bottle of Moët in the other, and two spots of livid crimson burned in her usually pale face. She clutched the table to steady herself before sliding into the empty seat. 'So, what's going on? Which hot guys have you two been eyeing up?'

Oh Lord, Hilly was pissed! Libby was taken aback because the senior agent was a total control freak and always very po-faced when her colleagues over-indulged on nights out. Her desk was neat, her record keeping was second to none and her clothes were always perfectly pressed and co-ordinated. The long flight and heat must have been too much for her. Catching Libby's eye, Janine pulled a face.

'I need the loo, again,' Janine said quickly and with great presence of mind. 'I seem to pee nonstop these days. Yet another joy of being up the duff.'

She rose heavily to her feet, waving away Libby's offer to escort her and, protesting that she was fine, waddled away through the busy bar.

'Christ,' said Hilary once Janine was out of earshot. 'You'd think that nobody ever had a baby before.' Sloshing more champagne into her glass, she added, 'Do you ever think about having kids?'

Libby shook her head. 'Whoa there! I'm not ready for that yet. My sister and her friends talk about it a lot but they've got a few years on me.'

'Yeah, that stuff can wait a while for me, too. I'm concentrating on my career right now.' She leaned forward confidingly and winked at Libby. 'In fact, between you and me, I'm pretty sure Tom's going to make a big announcement soon.'

In spite of herself Libby was curious. 'Really?

About what exactly?' She hoped for a second that he could be about to tell the company that they were together.

'About who's been chosen for senior partner, of course!' Hilary rolled her eyes.

'Oh.'

'You must know that job's been under consideration since Mike left?'

Libby did know. From the moment the vacancy had been announced it was all everyone had been talking about.

'And you think Tom might choose you?'

Hilary nodded. 'I don't *think*. I *know* he's going to choose me. And do you know why?'

Libby did not know. Hilary might be good at her job (although the word '*anal*' did spring to mind) but she totally lacked Kyle's dynamism and creative flair. Tom would have to be mad to choose Hilly over Kyle but since Hilary was staring at her expectantly she shook her head dutifully.

'It's not just because I'm the best at my job,' Hilary crowed, 'although obviously I am!' She leaned forward and dropped her voice conspiratorially. 'No, the reason why I know I'm definitely getting that promotion is because it'll mean Tom and I will have to work even more closely together.'

Libby was so lost that even a sat nav wouldn't have

helped. Why on earth would Tom want to work more closely with Hilary?

'Don't you get it?' Hilary asked, draining her glass. 'My God, I can't keep it a secret any more, but you must promise not to tell.' Leaning forward she fixed Libby with a triumphant smile. 'Tom's more than just my boss, Libby. Much, much more.'

Libby gulped as Hilary said the last words she expected to hear. 'Tom and I are an item!'

For a moment Libby didn't quite understand what she was hearing. Then she felt cold to her bones as the other woman's triumphant words sank in. Hilary was seeing Tom? Her Tom? The very same Tom who'd spent the past two months telling her that office relationships were a bad idea? In between making love to her and saying he adored her, of course.

Well, he was right, she thought, as fury bubbled up inside her like lava, Tom Richards was about to discover first hand that office romances were a very bad idea indeed – especially when you dated two of your staff at once!

'Don't look so shocked,' Hilary said petulantly. 'We've been together ages, actually. I would've thought it was obvious.'

Libby opened her mouth to tell Hilly exactly why she was so taken aback but then closed it again. Much as part of her would have loved to wipe the smug smile off her colleague's face the other part was still reeling from the shock of this unwelcome revelation. Besides, this hideous situation wasn't Hilary's doing. He'd played both women for complete idiots! Tom was very lucky he was the other side of the bar and still deep in discussion with the producers or he might already have been wearing his testicles as earrings.

Hilary's nut-brown eyes had narrowed. 'Are you all right? You've gone a very funny colour.'

Fanning herself, Libby muttered something about being hot and needing to get some fresh air – total nonsense seeing as she was already outside, but fortunately Hilary was far too sloshed to notice. Excuses made, Libby kicked off her glittery flip-flops and stomped down the beach to the water's edge, where the gentle lap of the waves and silver moonlight went some way towards soothing her.

How could she have been so stupid? No wonder Tom was so cagey about everyone else knowing they were seeing one another, going out of his way to meet her in restaurants the other side of the city or to book hotel rooms rather than invite her around to his flat. At the time she'd thought it was exciting and romantic but now, rose-tinted spectacles well and truly shattered, she could see things clearly at long last.

Talk about 'should've gone to Spec Savers'!

She dashed her tears away angrily with the back of her hand. Libby Forster didn't do crying. No way.

Hilary was welcome to him. In fact, the more she thought about it the more she was convinced they were made for one another. They went together perfectly, just like sickness and diarrhoea!

Libby was so lost in her miserable thoughts that she almost flew into orbit when a pair of warm arms wrapped themselves around her. She recognised those arms straight away and the spicy aftershave that drifted on the warm breeze.

What the bloody hell did Tom think he was playing at?

'Don't!' she snapped, shoving him away and leaping to her feet where, hands on hips, she glowered down at him. 'Don't you dare touch me!'

'Jesus, what's got into you?' Tom clutched his stomach and his handsome features twisted with pain. Oops. Fit and strong from kick boxing, Libby's shove had been rather more forceful than she'd anticipated.

'It's more a case of who *you've* been getting into!' she hissed.

Tom's dark eyes widened in a perfect picture of injured innocence. 'Babes, you're not making any sense.'

'Oh don't look at me like that,' she snapped, incensed that he was still playing her for a fool. 'Hilary has just told me everything. How you guys are an item and that you're about to promote her. Well, congratulations, Tom. I hope you'll both be really happy together!'

Tom's mouth hung open on its hinges. He looked identical to a Tango'd goldfish; if she hadn't been so angry Libby would have laughed.

'All that bollocks you spun me about being professional at work!' She shook her head, blond hair swinging across her face in perfect rhythm with her angry words. 'No wonder you wanted to keep our relationship a secret. You wouldn't have wanted your girlfriend to find out, would you?'

'Hilary's not my girlfriend!' Tom cried. 'She isn't,' he insisted when Libby raised a dubious eyebrow. 'At least she isn't any more. I broke things off with her a couple of weeks ago, I swear to God.'

'A couple of weeks ago?' Libby echoed incredulously. The guy was simply unbelievable. 'And that makes things all right, does it? Tom, we've been seeing each other for two months.'

But Tom wasn't listening. 'I broke it off with Hilly because of you, babe! I really, really like you. What we've got together is special, I know it is. I just didn't know how to tell her it was over.'

He reached out and took her hand but Libby shook him off.

'And you didn't think to tell me you had a girlfriend?' she hissed.

'I didn't want to lose you.'

She shook her head. 'Well, bad luck. You just have.'

Tom widened his eyes in what was usually his winning *I'm just a little boy* expression but suddenly Libby discovered that she was immune to it. That silly look on his face made her want to kick him, not forgive him.

'Come on, Libby Loo, don't be like this. I've finished things with Hilly, I promise I have. She's just having trouble accepting it.'

Libby stared at him in disbelief at how easily the lies rolled off his tongue. There was no way that Tom had broken things off. Hilary was many things but a good actress wasn't one of them. Besides, she'd been so drunk that if Tom really had finished with her she'd have been trying to stab Libby to death, not boasting about how loved up she was. Here was yet more evidence – as if she needed it – that Tom didn't have a clue about women. Libby's blue eyes narrowed. 'Hilary didn't sound to me as though she thinks it's over. Far from it. She thinks you're about to promote her so that you can work even more closely together. Where would she get an idea like that if not from you?'

Tom pulled a face. 'Look, how on earth do I know? Don't listen to a word she says, she's just trying to drive a wedge between us.'

'She's succeeded!' Libby said sharply. 'Hilly's

welcome to you because it's over between us.'

Tom began to plead and argue but she'd heard more than enough from him already. Turning on her heel, Libby strode away from him, her strong legs powering her back up the beach and towards the bar. Honeyed light spilled on to the sand and the tinkling sound of laughter rose on the gentle breeze but she couldn't face being in company, not while it felt as though someone was dragging barbed wire through her heart. Inside the bar everyone was happy, couples were holding hands or whispering together, and she didn't think she could bear it right now. Nor could she take having to face another dose of Hilary and her jubilant drunken boasting.

Feeling sick and angry, Libby turned left and headed into the hotel's lush tropical gardens. There, all was silent save the chirrup of crickets and the muted notes of piano music drifting from the bar. The tranquillity was exactly what she needed to gather her thoughts. Slowing her pace and allowing her ragged breathing to calm down she began to rationalise in a desperate attempt to put everything into perspective. She ought to just look on it as a bit of fun that got out of hand and nothing more. There was no point in becoming upset over a man who was nothing but a lying, cheating scumbag!

Oh, and her boss as well.

Bollocks. Maybe she'd cross that bridge when she came to it.

Libby's heart rate was almost back to normal and her pulse was coming back down to earth when she spotted Kyle strolling through the gardens.

'What are you up to?' Libby called out, laughing when Kyle practically leapt out of his sandals.

'Christ! You scared me half to death.' Kyle palmed something quickly and put his hand behind his back. Then, looking more closely at Libby said, 'Hey? Are you OK? You look really tense. Has something happened?'

'Where do I start?' Libby sighed.

'That bad, huh?'

She nodded. 'Yeah, about as bad as it gets.'

Kyle looked sympathetic. 'Poor you. Do you want to tell me about it?'

'I'd rather not,' said Libby firmly. 'Anyway, it's nothing important. I'm just jetlagged.'

'I know just the thing to sort that out,' said Kyle, bringing his hand back round and opening his fist to reveal a tatty-looking roll-up. 'This'll take the edge off.'

Libby stared at him. 'Is that what I think it is?'

Kyle grinned. 'Depends what you think it is. If you think it's a joint then, yes. One of the gardeners gave it to me in return for my packet of Bensons. A fair swap, I'd say! Fancy a toke?'

Libby shook her head. 'Not for me thanks; my smoking days are long gone.'

'All the more for me then,' Kyle said, stuffing the joint into his pocket.

'You've seriously got a death wish. If Janine finds out you've been smoking cannabis she'll *really* kill you. You promised her that was all in the past.'

'Janine used to love a toke,' Kyle sighed. 'All right, Libby, I feel sufficiently guilty now. How about I smoke this as my last ever joint before fatherhood and you come along too and hang out for a bit?'

Libby wasn't convinced as to the wisdom of this idea. When Kyle had a drink or two he tended to get a bit wild, which wasn't the best idea with Janine on the warpath.

'Come on, you know you want to. It's got to be better than being cornered by Hilly. She's even more of a nightmare when she's pissed!'

Libby had no desire to be anywhere near Hilary. She might not like the woman but she wasn't proud about doing the dirty on her, however unintentionally. So against her better judgment, she followed Kyle through the gardens and back into the hotel, figuring that at least this way she'd be able to keep an eye on him.

'This'll do,' Kyle said, pushing open the door to a plush restroom just off the lobby. 'Everyone's in the bars or restaurants now.'

Some restroom, thought Libby, glancing around. You could have fitted all of her old flat in it and still have room left over. The carpets were vivid crimson and so deep that the pile swallowed her feet all the way to her ankles, the elaborate flock wallpaper gave the place depth and the basins were real marble and crowned with gold taps. While Kyle leaned out of the window and smoked what might or might not be a joint (and to be honest he just seemed delighted to be within puffing distance of nicotine) they chatted about everything under the sun, from the film and its success, to Libby's ambition to bungee jump into the Grand Canyon. Although Kyle could obviously tell she was upset, he was enough of a good friend not to press the issue and little by little she started to unwind. She could only pray that Tom wouldn't do anything stupid like inform Hilary about their relationship. Hilary held a grudge like nobody on earth – she'd once blanked Libby for a week just for borrowing her stapler without asking, so heaven only knew what she'd make of having her boyfriend borrowed!

'Come on, Lib, something's up. Sure you don't want a toke?' Kyle asked, waving the roll-up at her.

She shook her head. Just a whiff of the cloying smoke was enough to make her head spin and she had a feeling she'd really need her wits about her this evening. 'I'm fine.'

Kyle regarded her thoughtfully. 'Bollocks. You're so wound up you'll be chiming in a minute.'

Libby laughed. Kyle was a lovely guy but not the most discreet member of the team. Besides, she wasn't going to waste another breath on Tom.

'Never mind me, what on earth's going on with you and Janine? She was really agitated earlier.'

He rolled his eyes. 'God knows. Lately I can't do anything right – she's even accused me of having an affair with you.'

Libby stared at him in horror. 'I hope you set her straight.'

'I tried but she wouldn't listen. She kept on and on about how you're always slipping out of the office at odd times, texting like crazy on your mobile and instant messaging. She's convinced it's me you're talking to.'

'You? As if I'd have an affair with you!'

'Thanks, Lib, there goes my ego,' Kyle said ruefully. 'Who's the lucky guy?'

'None of your business, nosey! I *was* seeing someone but believe me it's well and truly over now.'

They sat in silence for a minute, Kyle smoking thoughtfully while Libby tried her hardest to figure out how she could convince Janine she wasn't having an affair with Kyle, without mentioning Tom. Einstein probably sussed out relativity more easily.

'I do appreciate how hard things must be for Jan,' Kyle said eventually. 'But I wish she'd share things with me a little. I really want to be there for her, if she'll let me. I really do love her, you know.'

Libby reached out and touched his hand. 'Why don't you try telling her that? I bet all she really wants is a little bit of reassurance that you still want her.'

'You reckon?'

'Definitely!' Libby said with a confidence she didn't quite feel. To be honest, she was rather shocked that Janine had even thought for a millisecond she'd have an affair with Kyle. No wonder she'd been so prickly. Gathering herself, she added, 'Look, you're staying in paradise for two whole weeks. What better place to spend some quality time together and get things back on track before the baby comes?'

'You're right!' Stubbing out the rest of the joint, Kyle leapt up from his seat with a broad smile. 'I shouldn't be sitting here wasting time smoking. I need to go and find Janine.'

'I think that's the most sensible thing I've heard you say all night,' Libby told him as they made their way through the restroom back towards the lobby. Her own relationship might be in tatters but at least she'd helped Kyle and Janine patch things up.

She'd get to heaven yet!

But as soon as they stepped out into the lobby she

realised that nothing would be as straightforward as it had seemed a moment before. A heavy tropical downpour was hammering on to the glass roof and everyone outside had come dashing in to escape the sharp needles of rain. The lobby was no longer empty but teemed with damp bodies gently steaming in the heat and shaking raindrops from their limbs. At the very moment Libby and Kyle abandoned their secret smoking lair, the entire Cast Away team was gathered in the lobby.

Talk about fate pulling a moonie! Libby had the sudden horrible feeling that she was descending very, very fast in an elevator. Even she could see that this looked bad. Very bad.

'You'd better have a bloody good reason for being alone in there with her!' Janine was shrieking. Her shrill voice shattered the tranquil atmosphere of the lobby and drowned the delicate notes of the piano. She couldn't have drawn more attention to herself if she'd stripped naked and started to tap dance across the checkered floor. Now the rest of the cast and all the other hotel guests in the lobby were staring too.

'Jan! Sweetheart, it's not what it looks like,' Kyle insisted, trying to take his girlfriend in his arms but she sidestepped neatly and dealt him a stinging blow around the face.

'It's *exactly* what it looks like! You weren't playing

tiddlywinks, were you?' Her voice went up an octave. 'I knew something was going on, I knew it!'

'For God's sake, nothing happened. I was having a secret smoke and Libby came with me.'

'You don't smoke. You gave up. Or is that something else you've lied about?' Janine spat. 'You're seeing Libby, I know it. I've seen the way you're always talking to her.'

'We're colleagues!' Kyle cried, exasperated. 'I have to talk to her. We work together, for Christ's sake!'

Tom strode forward, putting his arm around Janine's shaking shoulders.

'What the hell's been going on?' he demanded, his dark eyes bright with anger.

'Nothing.' Libby couldn't believe this was happening. The more she and Kyle protested their innocence the guiltier they looked. How bloody unfair was that? Especially when she knew that *she* wasn't the cheating party in the room.

'Don't lie to me! I know you've been secretly seeing him for ages,' Janine screeched. 'You've been waiting for a chance to get your hands on him.'

'That's rubbish,' Libby protested but Janine rounded on her, cheeks scarlet with fury.

'Libby, I know you've been seeing someone in secret. I've heard you whispering on the phone and seen you sneak off. Don't deny it!'

Libby couldn't deny it but neither could she explain how things really stood, not with Hilary there anyway.

'Calm down!' Kyle was pleading. 'This is really bad for the baby.'

'Like you give a toss about the baby,' shrieked Janine, tears pouring down her cheeks. 'You wouldn't be cheating on me if you did.'

Kyle shook his head. 'You're being so horrible lately who'd blame me if I was?'

There was a collective gasp of horror at this. Kyle always was one to open his mouth and put both size tens inside, which right now really wasn't such a great quality. While everyone else goggled at him Libby covered her face in mortification and wished the ground would open and gulp her up, a wish that increased a thousandfold when Tom leapt forward and punched Kyle in the face.

'You fucking little shit!' he roared. 'How dare you touch my girlfriend?'

At this, Hilary's mouth fell open, a shocked Kyle clutched at his bleeding nose and Janine bolted from the lobby wailing at the top of her lungs. Then all hell broke lose. Hilary was screaming at Tom and pummelling him with her fists; Kyle was dripping blood all over the floor and Janine's wailing could still be heard even above all this commotion. For a moment Libby just stood there totally shell-shocked, until the full force of the situation hit her.

It was a total and utter disaster. So far she'd broken up with her (cheating) boyfriend, upset one of her closest colleagues, probably ruined Kyle's relationship rather than help to sort things out and, judging by the evil looks that really should have laid her out on the marble floor, made a very dangerous enemy in Hilary.

And it was only the first day.

How on earth had her wonderful trip to paradise gone so wrong so quickly? It was as if she had a curse on her. Wherever she went, she created disaster.

'Why are you still here?' Hilary screeched at Libby. 'Just go away and leave us all alone. Can't you see? Nobody wants you here!'

With a sob, Libby turned on her heel and fled back towards the beach, her heart doing a bass jump all of its own.

Libby ran along the beach as fast as she could, her feet pounding into the firm sand alongside the water's edge and her breath coming in sharp, hard gasps. On and on she ran until her lungs burned and she could no longer tell whether her cheeks were damp with tears or perspiration.

When she couldn't run any further, Libby flung herself down on to the beach where she lay panting until her pulse started to slow and her breathing was under control. Then she sat with her knees hugged close to her chest and her arms wrapped tightly around them and stared out at the black and restless sea.

'What a bloody mess,' she said out loud.

Libby ground her knuckles into her eyes making stars and comets leap against her irises, and sighed wearily. Dating Tom had been a huge mistake. As usual she'd been too busy galloping through life to think about the consequences. When her sexy boss had asked her out she'd jumped straight in without really thinking – although to be fair her horoscope that day had been adamant that it was a good time to explore new relationships. And she'd checked three different papers just to make sure!

Eventually, Libby got up and continued to walk through the surf along the length of the beach. All was quiet except for the sigh of the waves and the endless chirp of unseen crickets. As she walked Libby felt the stresses of the past hour slip away. She'd go back in a bit and apologise to everyone, grovel to Hilary and explain what had really been going on to Janine. Tom would have to eat humble pie, preferably a bloody big slice, and then everything would go back to normal.

At least she hoped it would.

She needed to give everyone time to calm down. Libby walked along the deserted beach until she reached the boundary of the hotel. For a split second she hesitated – the concierge had been most insistent that it wasn't safe to venture beyond – before she threw caution to the wind and scrambled over the low wooden boundary fence. Bollocks to playing it safe! A bit of risk-taking was far more fun. Libby had travelled around the Far East in her gap year and thoroughly enjoyed every minute of it. Besides, it wasn't as though the next beach was totally empty. Just up from the tide's reach a large bonfire fantailed orange sparks into the darkness and filled the air with a smoky tang. A group of young people basked in its glow. Somebody was strumming a guitar while the others chatted leisurely and laughed.

Backpackers, thought Libby with a nostalgic pang, as bubbles of their conversation rose and fell on the breeze accompanied by the aroma of barbecued cooking meat. Her mouth watered in spite of the fact that she'd eaten an exquisite lime and fish stir fry only hours earlier. Nothing beat a good old beach barbie! Almost without thinking she started to head towards them, waving when they turned to look at her.

'Hey!' she called. 'Do you mind if I join you?'

'Sure thing,' a voice called back.

She recognised the accent – Aussies! Libby smiled to herself because the last time she'd been in Thailand she'd hooked up with a group of Aussies and Kiwis and they'd had the best laugh. Smoothing down her dress and running her fingers through her tangled hair, she ran over to join the group.

A few minutes later she was sitting by the fire with a bottle of Bud in one hand and a burger in the other, struggling to remember the names that were being fired at her like bullets. As she munched her food Libby listened to the backpackers debate whether to stay another day or move on to Bangkok. Her attention kept being drawn to the guy who was sitting slightly apart from the rest, totally absorbed in strumming his guitar.

Whoa, thought Libby as her heart did a cartwheel. *He is gorgeous*. With his shoulder-length blond curls, cheeks burnished with golden stubble and sleepy green eyes he reminded her of Matthew McConaughey. The way his hands held the guitar, so tenderly coaxing music from each trembling string, made her feel quite giddy. Sensing her gaze, the guy looked up and gave Libby a lopsided grin which lit up his face and buried a dimple in his cheek.

Heart thumping, she looked away hastily. For heaven's sake! What was she thinking? After today, *you're sworn off guys*, she told herself sternly. But her gaze, it seemed, was immune to pep talks and logic because it kept slipping back to him.

Get a grip, Libby ordered herself. *Guys are bad news, remember?*

As she was chatting about her last backpacking trip, the love god looked up, giving Libby a wicked grin. In spite of her resolution to abstain from all things male and sexy forever more, she found herself smiling back. 'You know Bangkok? So I take it you've been to Thailand before?'

'Do I come here often, you mean?' quipped Libby.

He raised an eyebrow. 'Well, do you?'

She laughed. 'Not as often as I'd like! I spent a month here a couple of years back and I absolutely loved it. I couldn't believe my luck when they sent me out here for the shoot. I know I'll be working most of the time, but I'm really hoping to spend some of it checking out the local flavour.'

'So you enjoy travelling?' he wanted to know, gently placing the guitar on to the sand and fixing those sea-green eyes on her.

'Absolutely!' Libby nodded. 'I spend every spare penny taking myself off to exotic locations. I'm always broke but my passport has loads of stamps.'

'If you like travelling, there's no place better than Australia. But then I'm biased. There's more to us than barbies and *Neighbours*, you know.'

Looking at him, his skin as burnished as if someone had dipped him in liquid gold, Libby totally agreed. Australia looked as though it had a great deal to offer!

'I'm Craig, by the way,' he said as he smiled, sensing her looking. His wavy blond curls, bleached from endless days in the sun, flopped across his eyes in such a cute way that Libby had to look away quickly. This pull of instant attraction was *not* what she needed right now.

Craig picked up his guitar again and strummed thoughtfully while the conversation turned to places that the others had visited. Libby made them laugh by telling the story about how, aged sixteen, she'd saved the money from her Saturday job to travel to Mumbai in search of Dash Suri. 'I spent a fortune and it turned out he lived in Delhi! My research hadn't been very thorough after all, and I'd spent a fortune trying to find him in a place where he'd never even been! My sister thought I was nuts,' Libby recalled. 'But that's Zoe for you: she likes to play it safe.'

'And you don't?' Craig asked, looking up from his guitar.

'Not particularly. I like a challenge.'

'So do we,' another backbacker chipped in. 'That's why I think we should give it a few more days and do this parachute jump before we move on.'

'Parachute jump?' Libby asked.

'We've been waiting three days to go but the weather's been too wet,' explained the backpacker sitting next to her, a burly looking guy with dreadlocks. 'I'm starting to think we should just give it up as a bad idea. I reckon we're jinxed.'

'The weather's looking much better for tomorrow, mate,' said Craig. Man, but his accent was cute! 'I think we should give it one more shot.'

'I don't know how you could even consider jumping out of a plane!' shuddered a backpacker. A slim, pale hand fluttered to her throat like a nervous moth and her brown eyes widened. 'I'd never dare.'

' 'Course you would,' Libby said to encourage her. 'There's nothing to it.'

'Oh really?' Craig raised an eyebrow. 'In that case Libby, why don't you join us?'

She laughed. 'I don't think so. That's my only day off and I fully intend to spend it lazing by the pool, thanks!'

'That's hardly what I'd call a challenge,' Craig said, his green eyes locking with hers. 'Come on, join us. Unless you're scared, that is?'

Scared? Hardly! Libby had almost lost count of all the parachute jumps she'd done. But, not wanting to sound like a show-off, she just said, 'I'm not scared, Craig. I'm just looking forward to some down time.'

'Who'd want to laze about on a beach when they could be jumping from a plane?' said the dreadlocked guy with a curl of the lip. 'Sheilas!'

'Come on, Libby,' Craig said again, and now his eyes glittered with challenge. 'I dare you.'

Oh, Lord. Those fatal words. For a second the sensible side of Libby battled with the crazy daredevil version, before giving up in despair. It had never really stood a chance.

'A dare, huh?' she said slowly. 'In that case, you're on.'

'Cool!' Craig grinned from ear to ear. 'I can't wait.'

Libby raised her chin. Let him assume she was a rookie. She'd show him! 'Neither can I,' she said. 'Bring it on.'

Even though she'd sworn to think things through from now on and be less impulsive, one small parachute jump couldn't really hurt.

Could it?

5

Why, oh why, did she always get herself into these situations?

Thirteen thousand feet above sea level and strapped into a full body harness that wouldn't look amiss in a bondage dungeon, Libby was beginning to question the wisdom of agreeing to this parachute jump. Standing by the open plane door she surveyed the acres of lush green forest and pure white beaches that lay a dizzying drop below. This part of Thailand's coast was a picture-perfect tropical paradise with spectacular waterfalls foaming down into warm turquoise waters. The ocean sparkled more brightly than an Asprey's window display.

'You all right there, Lib? It's not too late to change your mind, you know.'

A slow, honey-warm drawl interrupted her thoughts as Craig, six feet of lean bronzed surf muscle and shaggy blond ringlets, squeezed her shoulder gently. He'd spent most of the thirty-minute ride to the drop-off point lolling against the fuselage, grinning, cracking jokes and generally looking as though he was chilling out at a party rather than potentially on the brink of plunging to his death.

She shook his hand off. 'I'm fine, thanks.'

'Listen, it's OK to back out if you want,' Craig said, giving her a smile that crinkled the corners of his emerald eyes and made the freckles scattered across his bronzed cheeks dance. 'Seriously, I know you'd had a few beers when I dared you to join me and I wouldn't hold it against you if you didn't go through with jumping. It's pretty bloody scary, even when you've done it a few times.'

Libby glared daggers at him. 'I'm not scared of *jumping*,' she said scornfully. For a split second she toyed with the idea of telling him that she'd done her first parachute jump on her eighteenth birthday and done at least five more in the years since, but something about the patronising way that all the guys on the plane were looking at her – as though she were made of spun glass and about to shatter at any second – stopped her. It would be a slap in the face for them and a strike for sisterhood when she hurled herself into the cobalt-blue sky without so much as a gasp.

'You look scared stiff to me, doll,' chipped in the burly Aussie who was lining up third to jump.

'I'm fine,' she said, through teeth gritted so hard it

was amazing they didn't splinter. 'In fact, the sooner I'm out of this heap of a plane the happier I'll be.'

As she checked her chute and ran through the drill Libby couldn't help feeling that jumping out of a plane was preferable to bumping into her colleagues today. When she'd finally returned to the hotel last night the coast was clear and she'd been up so early to meet the Aussies that she'd not seen them this morning either. There'd been not a drop of blood in the lobby, a disgraced Kyle wasn't camping outside her bedroom door, and neither was she greeted by a horse's head deposited by the seething Hilary. Maybe everything was going to settle after all? Pook, the stern-faced trainer who'd spent most of the morning barking instructions at them in broken English, was now lining up the jumpers in their parachuting order like toy soldiers. Harnesses were tightened, helmets and earpieces secured and final instructions issued. Peering over Pook's shoulder at the drop to earth Libby's stomach fizzed with delicious excitement. Craig was going first.

'Now! Jump!'

The plane door was wide open and for a moment Craig teetered on the brink before giving Libby the thumbs up and leaping into the void.

'You!' Pook barked at her and obediently Libby shuffled forward to the doorway, gasping when the icy wind slapped her cheeks and whipped tears from her eyes. She pulled her googles down swiftly and took a deep breath. This was it.

'Don't waste your time, mate. She'll never do it,' jeered the loudmouth Aussie. 'Jeez, step aside, love, will you? Let the rest of us have a go. Or just jump – if you've got the guts, that is!'

'Oh, I've got the guts all right,' Libby snapped.

'Oh yeah? So prove it!'

The taunting words were like the proverbial red rag to a bull and Libby couldn't help herself. Her limbs seemed to take on a life of their own, ignoring her brain – which was waiting patiently for Pook's order – and suddenly she was stepping into nothingness, the rushing wind howling its displeasure and the land racing towards her as she tumbled into empty air.

Shit! What was she thinking? It was far too soon to jump! She was supposed to wait at least two minutes before taking her turn! If Libby hadn't known this already then she ought to by now, since Pook had been attempting to drill it into them all morning. Now she was free-falling so fast that Craig was racing up to meet her at a sickeningly swift pace.

With a mouth as dry as the silver sand below Libby tugged frantically at her parachute cord, hoping against hope that she could open her chute in time and

avert almost certain disaster. It might have worked too
if only Craig hadn't chosen that precise moment to do
exactly the same thing.

'No! No!' Libby yelled, but the air plucked the
words from her lips. Instantly she was tangled up in a
knot of parachute strings like a small fly ensnared in a
very sticky web; no matter how desperately she jerked
her body to try and release herself she only succeeded
in knotting up the delicate lines.

Oh God, this was bad. This was really bad. What
had she done?

As the wind filled their parachutes, Libby and
Craig veered wildly off course in a tangle of silks
and cord. The ground – which only moments ago had
seemed so far away – was now racing up to meet them
with such sickening speed that even she with her
steady head for heights started to feel giddy and faint.
They were only minutes away from disaster.

Pook was shrieking into her earpiece, probably
giving her valuable instructions, but since they were
all in Thai any advice he may have offered was totally
lost on Libby. Tears stung her ears and her throat
tightened with terror. Why, oh why, did she never
think things through? She was all for adrenalin rushes
but this was too much even for her. If only she'd kept
a cool head and ignored the smug Aussie's taunts then
she'd be drifting merrily down to the landing strip

rather than facing the fact that she was about to become a blob of Libby jam.

And poor Craig, too, none of this was his fault.

Bloody hell, Libby thought wryly as she continued to fight to free herself, *when that fortune-teller said I was a danger to men she wasn't joking! And she said to watch out in September . . .*

Although to be honest she'd truly thought this prophecy had been fulfilled last night. In her wildest dreams she hadn't been able to imagine things getting worse.

But the chaos of last night, it seemed, was only the beginning . . .

6

Plummeting through the sky with the earth hurtling towards her, Libby had never been more petrified. Forget the thrilling rush of adrenalin which sharpened the senses and piqued the nerves, this was something else entirely. Now, as she tugged the cord and desperately twisted her body from left to right in a vain attempt to disentangle herself from Craig, she felt faint with fear and her stomach was even more knotted than the parachute cords. It was no use. No matter what she did both parachutes were totally entwined. Libby had no steering and absolutely no idea how they were going to avoid crashing into the thick forest below.

Below, Craig was twisting round to look up at her and he was shouting something but his words were snatched away by the wind. He was gesturing as well but for the life of her Libby couldn't figure out what he was trying to say.

'I'm sorry! I'm sorry!' she half sobbed, half shouted.

Craig shook his head in frustration before waving his arm again towards the left.

In her earpiece Libby could hear Pook shrieking instructions in machine-gun rapid Thai. *'Kaang saai! Kaang saai!'* and almost wept with frustration because she had absolutely no idea what any of this meant.

Then, very unexpectedly, the speed of their drop began to slow as somehow Craig's chute caught a rogue current of tropical air, lifting them up and over the rainforest canopy. This change in speed and direction was deliberate, Libby realised, because it was too measured to be anything else. Craig had managed to gain control of the steering of both parachutes. They weren't plunging to their deaths after all!

Opening her eyes she saw that Craig's open parachute was guiding them both away from the rainforest and towards a white slither of beach. He was giving a thumbs up, which she weakly copied. Then Craig, who must have mastered the Thai words for right and left, was somehow managing to guide their knotted chuttes away from the razor-sharp treetops and down towards the powdery sand. To manage to manoeuvre their damaged chutes like this was nothing short of amazing. There was no time to think about anything else because the ground was racing up to meet them and with a thud she was down and rolling around and around on the beach.

Terra firma! Thank my stars! Libby could hardly believe that she was back on the ground and apparently with nothing broken. If it weren't for the fact she'd get a mouth full of sand she would have knelt down and kissed the beach, Pope style. Hell, she'd do it anyway. Who cared?

'I'm alive!' she shouted at the top of her lungs. Then gave the floor a smooch.

'Woo hoo!' shouted Craig from somewhere behind her. 'We live another day!'

Hearing his words made the enormity of what had almost happened strike Libby like a punch to the solar plexus. Her stupid, reckless behaviour and childish inability to resist a dare or ignore a taunt had almost killed her; worse than that, because she had risked Craig's life too with her silly antics. She started to cry as the adrenalin ebbed away. Her surroundings blurred as she sank to her knees, sobbing and gasping.

'Hey, what's this?' Disentangling himself from his parachute he strode towards her and scooped the sobbing and shocked Libby into his arms. 'Shush, now. Don't cry.' But she couldn't stop. There she trembled and wept her heart out while his strong hands cupped her face and smoothed her hair back from her damp cheeks.

'Ssh,' he said softly as he wiped her tears away with his thumb, 'it's OK.'

'It isn't,' Libby choked. 'I nearly killed you!'

'But you didn't. I'm fine. We both are,' Craig insisted, but Libby was totally beyond reason now and nothing he said could calm her. All she could think about was just how close they'd come to not making it. They'd been a hair's breadth away from disaster and it was all her fault.

'I nearly got us killed!' she choked. 'Why don't I ever stop to consider what might happen?'

'I get the feeling that if you did you wouldn't be you.' Craig grinned, those sparkly green eyes crinkling at her. 'Don't go changing, Lib! Seizing life with both hands is bloody sexy if you ask me!'

Libby wasn't asking Craig. She was far too busy madly prodding him from head to foot to make sure that he hadn't broken any bones. Finally, laughing and protesting that he was far too ticklish to bear any further inspection, Craig captured her slim wrists in his hands to stop the onslaught.

'Hey. I'm fine!' He laughed, twinkling down at her. 'In fact, I'm buzzing. That was such a rush, I should be thanking you. That was the jump of my life.'

Libby stared up at him. Was he insane? She'd almost got them killed and he was thanking her?

'Remember that really cool bit where we were over the trees? The leaves practically tickled my butt!' Craig was saying, his eyes shining with enthusiasm.

'The bit where it looked like we might be impaled, you mean?' Libby thought she'd probably be having nightmares about being skewered on a treetop for a very long time.

'Like I'd have let that happen,' he said as he grinned.

In spite of her shock, Libby started to giggle partly because his enthusiasm was so infectious and partly because it was crazy he was grateful! If he wasn't totally lit up with the thrill of it all she'd have thought he was taking the mickey. She shook her head in disbelief. This guy was even more of an adrenalin junkie than she was!

Gently helping Libby to her feet – easier said than done seeing as her legs had all the strength of soggy Weetabix – Craig pulled her close and wrapped his arms around her.

'You're some wild girl, Libby,' he murmured, his face so close that his eyelashes practically brushed hers.

And then he was kissing her and, caught up in the moment and the relief that they were OK, Libby found she was kissing him back. At first it was a kiss as soft as the brush of a butterfly's wings, so gentle to begin with as his hands came up and held her face while she closed her eyes in delicious anticipation. Then she melted beneath the warmth of Craig's mouth on hers and felt the muscles of those strong arms rippling as he held her close. For a moment Libby lost herself in the sensation, felt herself dissolve like Ambre Solaire in the hot Thai sunshine as his hands slipped from her face to caress her body while she in turn slid her hands beneath his T-shirt and felt the taut muscles of his chest.

Oh wow! she thought as his lips moved to the tender skin of her neck. This was amazing. Maybe she should dice with death more often? Kissing Craig certainly beat the furtive assignations with Tom in the stationery cupboard.

Tom! Libby's eyes flew open and suddenly everything felt wrong, out of kilter like a tune being played in the wrong key. What on earth was she thinking, kissing a near stranger when she'd only just broken up with her boyfriend? And more than that, what about being a danger to men? If she'd ever needed proof that Angela's prophecy was spot on then surely this near miss was it? She should be running a mile from poor Craig, not snogging him.

She pulled away and shook her head. 'Sorry. I shouldn't have done that.'

'Hey, don't be sorry. I'm not.' Craig gave her a slow, sexy smile and in spite of her resolve Libby felt her insides cartwheel. 'In fact I—' But Craig stopped; he studied Libby's face. 'What's wrong? Have I offended you, Lib?'

He looked so worried and so sweet that Libby could hardly bear to look at him.

'No, of course not,' she said quickly. 'But I don't know what came over me just then. Maybe it was the shock?'

Those merry green eyes twinkled. 'Maybe? And maybe not, but anyway I liked it. Jeez, Lib, you are something else!'

You don't know the half of it, Libby thought darkly. 'I didn't mean to do that,' she said.

'Do what? Kiss me or nearly kill me?'

'Both!' She buried her face in her hands. 'It's all a disaster.'

Craig looked a bit taken aback. 'No one's ever told me my kissing's a disaster before!'

Oh Lord, her face was back in that blast furnace again. 'Craig, that wasn't at all what I meant.'

But Craig was laughing now, his head thrown back and the strong muscles of his throat rippling with mirth. 'I'm teasing you! I think we probably both got a bit swept up in the rush of it all. Whoa, what a day.'

'Hmm,' said Libby, who was still feeling rather travel sick from this particular ride. She was all for adrenalin rushes but sometimes a girl could have too much of a good thing.

And that went for men as well as for parachuting!

In the distance Libby saw Pook and the rest of the

team running over, desperate to see if they were OK. In an hour's time she'd be dropped off at her hotel and Craig would continue onwards with his travelling companions. No doubt they'd be setting off tomorrow for the next spot on their itinerary and she'd never see him again. Which could only be a good thing.

It was best for the whole male gender if she kept her distance.

7

Although it was only early in the morning and a mist had wrapped itself along the seashore like a fluffy white scarf, a golden balloon sun was already rising in the sky and sending its heat down to earth. As Libby headed across the sand towards a cordoned-off section of the beach she could feel her skin begin to tingle and was glad to be wearing sapphire-blue cotton trousers and a loose white cotton shirt rather than the skimpy shorts and bikini tops that other crew members were wearing. She had no desire to end up sunburned and miserable.

OK then, end up sunburned. She was already miserable.

Kyle had blanked her at dinner last night, Hilary was nowhere to be seen (out plotting revenge some-where?) and as for Tom, well he was conspicuous by his absence, too. There'd been no grovelling apology notes pushed under her door, no pleading messages on her mobile and a distinct lack of 'I'm sorry I was a dick' bouquets delivered by the concierge. Not that any of this would have made the slightest bit of difference after the way he'd lied to her and Hilary, but it would have made Libby feel a whole heap better to think that Tom was suffering.

A danger to men, eh? Bloody right she was if she ever got the chance to show Tom how angry he'd made her. At least when Craig jumped he'd had a parachute. In Libby's opinion it was high time Tom tried some extreme sports, too. Cordless bungee jumping would be a good start . . .

'Water? Fruit? You buy? Yes?'

A small Thai girl pushing a small cart laden with bottles of water and slices of melon approached Libby with a beaming smile. Libby was totally unable to resist the child. She was so cute with her shiny jet-black bob and gap-toothed grin. Besides, she'd need a bottle of water to keep herself hydrated today, she thought as she bought one and stowed it away in her rucksack.

Flashing her crew card at the cordon she wove her way through a sea of trailers to the set. Around her scuttled extras dressed in jewel-coloured harem pants and lavishly embroidered bras, or muscled men dressed in snow-white loincloths, slicing at the air with vicious scimitars. She had cast all these people and as she stood watching the scene come to life Libby felt a tingle of pride and excitement. This was the bit she loved most about her job, seeing the story start to unfold and the script come to life as the extras donned their costumes and the makeup artists got to work. It was like magic and this film, a romantic musical with big set pieces and a vast wardrobe budget, certainly had more than its fair share of the budget ring-fenced for elaborate costumes and glitzy sets. Maybe that was one of the reasons they'd decided to plump for Trinity Duval rather than someone more expensive?

All around her was a plush blend of influences from India, China, Cambodia and a mish-mash of the rest of Southeast Asia. Fern would love it; it was just like the sitting room of her flat! Actually, talking of Fern, she used to date Luke Scottman, Trinity's latest squeeze, when she was at uni. That was long before he'd been rocketed into stardom and become one half of *Scinity* – the nickname that the tabloid press had given Hollywood's latest golden couple. She'd have to call Zoe a bit later to see what gossip she could wheedle out of her sister. From what Libby recalled Luke had seemed a pretty down-to-earth kind of guy. What was he doing with a woman who was rumoured to be more demanding than the queen? Apparently, she insisted that anyone she came into contact with had to be skinny because she'd read that fat was contagious. Maybe it was all just PR and bad press.

'Is this water organic?' shrilled a voice that had all the grace of nails scraping down a chalkboard. 'Don't let the sun shine on my face!'

Well, that answered the *bad press* question, thought Libby wryly as she leapt aside and narrowly avoided being trampled by Trinity Duval. A vision in pink silk which clung to every bone of her slender body, Trinity strode through the crowds of crew and extras with all the confidence of Moses parting the Red Sea – although Moses probably didn't have a mane of shimmering fake blond hair and boobs like cantaloupe melons. Mesmerised – she'd never seen a real fake pair, so to speak – Libby watched as Trinity ordered all and sundry about, demanded a change of costume at the eleventh hour and then threw a temper tantrum because the sunshade she'd requested had yet to materialise. The scene was only a brief one where the lead character had her face washed and then made up for the prince by the harem girls, but from the way Trinity complained you'd have thought they were trying to exfoliate her face with a scouring pad.

'Get my parasol!' she was shrieking, leaping from her bed of cushions and shielding her face with a pillow. 'Don't you realise just how sensitive my skin is?'

The assistant director, a small nervous-looking man (although to be fair, Libby thought Trinity's yelling would have made even James Cameron quail), tried his hardest to placate the actress but to no avail; she wasn't going to put up with such shoddy treatment. No sunshade, no filming.

'And I absolutely refuse to be filmed without make-up on,' she demanded so loudly that Libby's eardrums winced. 'My contract states quite clearly that I will only appear with makeup on.'

'But it's in the script: the Prince's harem slaves paint your face,' protested the assistant director, his own face as white as the extras' robes. 'It's part of the story!'

'Well not any more, it isn't,' Trinity said firmly. 'I want my makeup artists to apply a base first. Then the extras can apply some more if they really have to. But I'm not appearing on screen with naked skin.'

And with this she leapt to her feet and stormed from the set in a swirl of pink chiffon and outrage. Libby's chin nearly hit the sand. She'd never seen such a tantrum. Her strops made Mariah Carey look like Mary Poppins!

Luke Scottman was welcome to her – the guy must be nuts.

'Jeez, what a temper,' remarked Tom who'd managed to creep up unnoticed during Trinity's outburst. He smiled at Libby as though the events of the other night had never happened. 'Thank God, we don't have to deal with her. Any luck with casting the extras for the crowd scene?'

For a second Libby was absolutely lost for words – something that her sister would find very hard to believe because normally she chattered like a magpie on speed – but right now she really couldn't utter so much as a squeak. Firstly, she could hardly believe that Tom had the gall to saunter over and chat to her like nothing had ever happened, as though he'd never two-timed her with Hilary and totally wrecked her credibility with the team, and secondly because Dash Suri had just arrived on the set and whizzed her back ten years quicker than you could say 'Tardis'. Suddenly she was a lanky teenager again!

'Are you listening to me?' Tom asked. 'Will you stop gawking at film stars for long enough to actually give *your boss* an update on your plans for casting the crowd scene?'

Oh, right. He was going to pull rank was he? Well, fine, thought Libby, two could play the professional card. Yanking her attention away from the vision of male beauty that was almost within touching distance, she tried her hardest to listen politely to Tom as he lectured her about fees and contracts and time limits. But despite her good intentions it seemed that her eyeballs had suddenly become Dash magnets and no matter what she did they kept sliding from Tom and pinging right back to the movie stars. Maybe she'd get to speak to Dash if she hung around long enough?

'Libby! Hey, Libby!'

Libby was dragged back to reality by Tom yelling at her and snapping his fingers beneath her nose in a really rude fashion.

'You haven't listened to a word I've said. For Christ's sake! You're here to work, Libby, not indulge some pathetic teenage crush!'

His voice was so loud that several heads snapped round to stare. Libby's cheeks flamed. Even Dash gazed in her direction before turning his attention back to the script he'd been studying. Libby was mortified: Tom had never, ever raised his voice to her before. With a jolt she realised he was actually angry with her for what had happened in the hotel lobby. Of all the bloody cheek. She wasn't the cheating, lying git in this equation! In fact, so far as she recalled, she was the injured party here and was the one who was supposed to be furious with him!

Libby was just about to open her mouth and tell Tom exactly what she thought of him when the fascinated gaze of the onlookers stopped her in her tracks.

Tom might have wrecked her love life but there was no way she was going to let him ruin her professional one, too. Clamping her mouth shut and biting the inside so hard that she tasted blood (she could now add making her self-harm to her increasingly long list of grievances against Tom) Libby forced herself to ignore her sense of injustice and listen. Once he'd finished bawling her out for not paying sufficient attention to him, Tom finally got to the point. The reason he was so stressed wasn't really down to Libby, or at least not directly: it appeared that half of the casting team had disappeared.

Libby stared at him. 'What do you mean, disappeared?'

Tom pressed his palms against his temples in despair. 'Exactly that. They've vanished. I haven't seen Hilly since she stormed off last night, and Kyle says that Janine's gone missing, too.'

Libby was horrified. 'But she's five months pregnant!'

'Never mind that, she and Kyle were supposed to be doing the martial arts casting for the major fight scenes.'

'The milk of human kindness just went sour,' muttered Libby under her breath but Tom was into his stride now and not interested in listening to what she had to say.

'Obviously Kyle's in no state to go out casting at the moment. And even if he was, he couldn't work with you; it would look far too incriminating if Janine turns up,' he was saying, with all the tact of a bull rampaging through Wedgwood's workshop. 'So there's nothing for it, you'll have to do the casting for the fight scenes yourself.'

'But nothing's happened between me and Kyle!' Libby protested. How come she was the bad guy all of a sudden? 'I was sleeping with *you*, remember? I was the one who *wasn't* called Hilary!'

'Look, I don't give a monkey's about all that right now,' Tom snapped, his brown eyes glittering with impatience. 'All that matters is not ballsing up this job and getting this casting done properly. I'm beyond caring who does what and who did what as long as this job gets done.' He fixed her with a steely glare. 'I guess the question is are you up to doing a major casting on your own?'

Oh wow! Talk about every cloud having a silver lining! Libby felt a little zizz of excitement shoot through her nervous system. She'd been longing to have the chance to prove herself by taking on a solo casting, now it seemed she was being handed this opportunity on a plate. OK, so the downside was that everyone saw her as a boyfriend-stealing-floozie but surely once she found Janine she could put the record straight?

'Well?' Tom was asking. 'Are you up for it? Or do I need to call London and fly someone else out?'

Libby raised her chin. So what if all she knew about casting fight scenes could be written on a postage stamp and still have room left over? Of course she could do it! How hard could it possibly be?

'I'll do it,' she said firmly. 'No problem.'

'Good,' said Tom curtly. 'Just make sure you don't muck it up. Our reputation depends on getting this right. Christ, this heat is unbearable,' he added, mopping his face. 'I'll be glad to get back to the UK.'

Tom couldn't take the sun. His nose was already pink and peeling and the tips of his ears were starting to glow. Although she still thought he was an utter knob for what he'd done, Libby had a kind heart and didn't like to think of him getting heatstroke. And on a selfish note that would leave her as the sole casting agent and, ambitious as she was, Libby didn't think she was *quite* up to that just yet.

'Have my hat,' she said, whipping off the baseball cap and shaking her thick blond hair over her shoulders. 'And keep hydrated, too. Here, take my water. You look like you need a drink.'

She handed him the bottle she'd bought earlier from the Thai girl and although it was rather warm from being in her bag, Tom gulped it down thirstily.

'No, keep it,' she said when he offered to return it. 'I think you need it more than I do.'

'Thanks, Lib.' Tom finished the water and gave her a rueful smile. 'You're a great girl, you really are. Look, about this thing with Hilly. I—'

'Tom, please don't start!' Libby raised both her

hands in protest and took an involuntary step away. 'Let's just concentrate on getting this job done, shall we?'

He sighed. 'If that's what you want.'

'It is; it really is,' Libby said firmly. Then, changing the subject quickly, because she *really* didn't want to go down this emotional cul-de-sac, she pointed to a large butch man who was trying to calm Trinity. 'Hey, isn't that Eastwood Jones? The action films guy? What on earth is he doing here?'

Tom shook his head, which looked rather comical since he was wearing Libby's pink baseball cap. 'You really don't read my memos, do you? If you did you'd know he's just signed up to direct the film. Come on, I'll introduce you.'

Libby's eyes widened with surprise. Eastwood Jones, six foot two of shaven-headed solid brawn who could easily take Vin Diesel on and win, was the last candidate on earth she would have imagined directing a historical romance! Even now, as Libby could see Trinity still complaining in the distance, Paris Hilton handbag dog tucked under her bony arm and several minions scuttling in her wake, he was stamping on his script and kicking his director's chair.

'Maybe this isn't the best time to meet him?' she said nervously as Tom pulled her over. 'He looks a bit stressed.'

'This is nothing,' said Tom cheerfully. 'In fact, this is him in a good mood. Come on, you should meet him seeing as you're casting the few action scenes.'

Libby gulped. Eastwood Jones looked like he munched on twenty-four-year-old casting assistants for lunch and picked their bones clean for dinner. Call her fussy, but she quite wanted to live to see twenty-five.

'Stupid bloody cow!' roared Eastwood, attacking the director's chair with his army boot. 'Won't follow the script because her face is too precious? Everyone knows it's so full of Botox it should carry a fucking health warning! Those extras should be refusing to go near *her*!'

In spite of being rather nervous of the kicking feet and flailing limbs, Libby couldn't help giggling. Catching her eye the director's lips started to twitch and moments later he was laughing and shaking his head.

'Fuck me, what was I thinking working on a bloody historical movie with a load of hormonal actresses? I knew I should have stuck to action movies!'

'I loved *Lethal Weaponry*,' Libby said, unable to help herself because it really was one of her favourite all-time films. 'The stunts were incredible. The bit when they base jump from the Empire State building was spectacular. I'd love to do that!'

Eastwood Jones's boot paused, mid-air. 'I wish the

leading man had been so keen. What a girlie wuss he was! I had to hire a stunt double.'

Libby decided to let the sexist comment go. That famous temper was still simmering and she had no desire to bring it back to boiling point. Once Tom had made the introductions and Eastwood had complained bitterly about having to deal with namby-bloody-pambies, smashing his fist into a giant coolbox of drinks as he did so, the conversation turned to the action sequences in *The Indian Prince and I*.

'The only bloody thing I've got to look forward to in this bloody pansy fest are those epic fight scenes,' said Eastwood woefully. 'Loads of soppy stuff and just a few fights to really get our teeth into.'

'Libby's going to be casting those scenes,' said Tom. 'That's what we need to talk to you about. Your vision is really important to us.'

At just the thought of a good old bit of gore and violence, Eastwood Jones lit up like a Christmas tree.

'It's going to be like something out of *Crouching Tiger, Hidden Dragon*. I want hundreds of extras all tightly choreographed and moving together in perfect harmony like one huge awesome being! And they must be young men, too, no one over thirty, and well muscled and handsome. I want young gods with bodies that would make Adonis consider plastic surgery!'

'That sounds like a clear vision,' Tom said smoothly. 'Shouldn't be a problem at all, should it, Libby?'

Libby gulped. The irony of her casting assignment did not escape her. She was going to have to scout for loads of fit guys. So much for taking Angela's advice and staying away from men. She was going to have to tread very, very carefully and be every inch the professional. But she could do it? Of course she could, and she'd prove to everyone just what a good casting agent she really was.

Lifting her chin a fraction she fixed the director with her brightest and most confident smile.

'It'll be no problem at all. I can hardly wait to get started.'

She genuinely couldn't wait. After all, what could really go wrong?

Twenty-four hours later Libby was sitting beneath a large sun umbrella, tapping notes into her trusty Macbook and congratulating herself on a job well done. She'd spent the past six hours watching a stream of young Thai guys with more muscles than Rick Stein's seafood restaurant strutting their stuff and performing *Matrix*-style moves across the beach.

It was a dirty job but someone had to do it!

Libby shut the Mac down and drained the dregs of her rather warm Diet Coke. Yuck! She could hardly wait to get back to the hotel and have a long cold drink. She was hot and sticky, too, from being on the set for ages and the thought of plunging into the sea was irresistible. After putting in the hours today and not even stopping for lunch she reckoned she'd earned a break, especially seeing as she'd handled everything on her own. She'd loved the challenge and the buzz of being the one to make the ultimate decisions – but she'd thought Tom might have popped over just to check she was OK. He hadn't even texted or called.

'Excuse me, little one, but I very much like to audition for part in film.'

A soft voice interrupted her daydream about becoming a high-powered Alexis Colby-style career woman. Glancing up from her folders, Libby saw an elderly Thai man with his head bowed and hands pressed together. His skin was as lined and folded as chamois leather, his eyes soft and dark as molasses and, as he regarded her, he dipped his head in a gesture of respect.

'Please?' he repeated in a voice as soft and as restful as the whispering waves. 'May I audition for part of noble warrior?'

Taken aback, Libby could only stare at him. What on earth was she supposed to say to this? The old dude looked like Methuselah's big brother and much as she would have loved to cast him as a wise sage or mentor he couldn't possibly be considered as a kick-boxing warrior. Heaven only knew what damage the old guy would do to himself if he tried to do a kung fu kick! He'd need a hip replacement within seconds.

Deciding a tactful approach was probably required, Libby pointed out that unfortunately the casting was completed and all the parts already filled. Surely that had to be less of a blow than telling him he was just too old?

'I'm afraid we've already cast our warriors,' she finished gently.

The old man raised his chin. 'But I am Panom Yeerum! I am real warrior! True warrior! Little one, I insist, I must audition.'

She stared at him. A real warrior? Maybe about a hundred years ago!

'I fight!' Panom insisted, striking a Karate Kid-style pose. As he attempted to kick his skinny leg into the air, his joints snapping like pistol shots, Libby realised she needed Panom like Bill Gates needed an overdraft. This guy was bonkers!

'I'm sorry, Mr Yeerum,' she said firmly. 'Like I said, we've finished the casting now. Maybe you could try out for the crowd scene another day?'

His hand rose to his mouth in a gesture of disbelief. 'Lady, you not mean this. I do another for you. I do Vin Diesel, yes?'

'No!' Libby said quickly but it was too late. Panom was now busy shuffling across the sand with flailing fists and a gurning expression on his wrinkly face. Suddenly Libby totally understood how Simon Cowell must feel in *X Factor* auditions.

'Well?' he panted when he finally came to a stop. 'Yes?'

She shook her head. 'Sorry, Panom. It's still a no.'

'You not like my Vin Diesel? No matters. I also Schwarzenegger! *I'll be back!*'

Libby couldn't help laughing at this because this

tiny, frail-looking guy was about as similar to Arnold Schwarzenegger as she was to Nicole Scherzinger.

'Sorry,' she told him, 'but you really won't be back because there isn't a part for you.'

Panom fixed her with big beseeching eyes sadder than the Andrex puppy on a very sad day. 'But to be in this film is big dream! Is my only dream.'

Libby stared down at her sandals in despair. Dream was about right. There was no way she was going to cast this crazy old dude as a ninja; her career in casting would be over before it had even begun. Still, she couldn't help feeling sorry for him. Panom might be nuttier than a Walnut Whip but Libby had to admit he'd given this his best shot and she felt quite unable to bear his disappointment. Still, being a professional, this was exactly what she would have to do. Panom Yeerum could beg for a thousand years, it wouldn't make any difference. He was too old to play a ninja.

'But little one—' Oh, Lord! Now he'd fallen to his knees and was actually pleading, his hands folded together in prayer! The time for tact was over. She was going to have to be blunt. Some people just couldn't take no for an answer.

'Look, Panom,' she said slowly. 'I really appreciate how difficult this is for you but I really can't cast you in this scene. For one thing, you're far too old and for another I already have the forty people that the director required. Even if you were right for the part – which I'm afraid you're not – we already have all the people we need.'

She was Simon Cowell's evil twin.

She braced herself for a torrent of anger or yet more pleading but surprisingly Panom seemed to take this rejection in his stride. Slowly and creakily he managed to clamber back to his feet again before drawing himself up to full height with a quiet dignity.

'And so it is,' he said slowly, 'that the needs of the many to the few must be considered as though an elephant to a mouse.'

'Err . . . right,' said Libby.

'As the sun rises for one so it must set on another,' Panom added with a shrug. 'The dark and the light are but two faces of the same coin.'

Wow. That was profound, if a little odd, Libby thought as Panom shuffled away. He'd suddenly seemed very philosophical about not being cast. Maybe he was some kind of guru or perhaps a mystic leader?

Either that or he was insane.

The film world was full of bizarre characters and she really needed to stop being surprised by it. Just look at Trinity Duval. Why should the extras be any less crazy?

And talking of crazy, now Eastwood Jones was heading towards her with all the gentleness of a heat-seeking missile. His giant redwood legs pounded across the set and judging by the puceness of his face and the way his ham-like hands were clenched into fists, this wasn't a social visit. Shit! Libby wracked her brains to think of something – anything – she could have done to upset the volatile director but drew a total blank. Oh, bollocks, that was even worse! She'd have no time to think of a defence and would be crushed into Libby crumbs within minutes. As her adrenalin levels soared, Libby comforted herself with the thought that dealing with the volatile director could double as a new variety of extreme sport.

'Where's Tom?' Eastwood demanded, slamming his hands on to the table and making Libby and the laptop practically take off into outer space. 'I've been trying to call him all day, godammit, and he hasn't answered. Do you know where he is?'

For a second Libby was sorely tempted to drop Tom in it. Couldn't happen to a nicer man. The guy could show Pinocchio a thing or two about fibbing, and now he'd gone AWOL on her. Just a few words from her were all it needed for Tom to get his just deserts. But the bad karma would take years to pay back, and she was already struggling with her overdraft!

She took a deep breath. 'He's just left. He said something about having to rush off on urgent business.'

Eastwood was scowling. 'I'm not paying him to *rush off*. I'm paying him to be here when I need him and to be my head of casting. Where's he gone anyhow?'

Libby had no idea. He'd looked a bit rough earlier and he might have spent the day in bed. But more likely he was sipping cocktails in the hotel bar, back to his usual slick self in a crisp linen suit and Armani sunglasses.

Git.

'No idea, huh?' boomed Eastwood.

She shook her head while her eardrums trembled. 'I'm pretty junior so Tom doesn't always tell me what he's up to.'

Actually, that was true, wasn't it? She wasn't directly fibbing to the director, a thought which perked Libby up immensely. Hopefully her angels were watching this and would chalk it up on some heavenly score-board somewhere. Then she could cash in her spiritual brownie points when she most needed them.

'The casting's going well though,' she said swiftly, before the director had time to become even more irate. 'I've sourced all the extras for the fight sequence and I'm really pleased.' She waved her hand in the direction of the folders. 'Would you like to have a look?'

'No, no, I'm sure you've done a great job,' Eastwood said, giving her a Hollywood-white smile so bright that Libby would still be seeing it an hour later. 'Seeing as we're missing Tom, you'll be in charge of the casting now, won't you?'

Would she? Excitement started to fizz through Libby's bloodstream. She supposed he was right. Awesome!

'Certainly,' she said, hoping her voice was steady even though mentally she was flick-flacking across the beach at the thought of this unexpected opportunity.

'In which case,' the director continued, clapping a meaty hand on to her shoulder, 'we'll forget about Tom and you can deal with all the paperwork.'

'Paperwork?' Libby echoed. 'For what?'

'For hiring my great find, of course! The man you're going to be working closely with for the next few weeks.' Eastwood beamed. 'Ah, here he is at long last.'

A figure, long-limbed and moving with a fluid grace, was heading towards them. He was dressed in loose black trousers and a white vest top which showed off the sculpted lines of his muscular chest to perfection. The glare of the sun was so bright behind him that it was impossible to make out his features, yet there was something rather familiar that made Libby pause. She must have been out in the sun too long because for a split second there she could have sworn it was . . .

'Libby, meet our new martial arts expert,' hollered Eastwood, each word blasting into her thoughts like cannon fire. 'You'll be impressed because what this boy doesn't know about Thai boxing just ain't worth knowing!'

Libby reached for her Raybans and slid them on, not wanting this man's first impression to be of her screwed-up face. Once her vision was shaded though, she gasped and her hands flew to her mouth. 'Here he is,' the director said proudly as the new recruit joined them. 'Our very own kick-boxing king!'

No way? It couldn't be! It was impossible.

Why, oh why, was fate determined to flip her the bird today? This guy had already seen the very worst of her and just about lived to tell the tale.

Craig!

Fan-flipping-tastic, she thought as her treacherous stomach danced the conga. She was off men; she was a danger to them, remember? And besides, she'd just decided to focus one hundred per cent on her career.

So enforced proximity to this man was *exactly* what she didn't need. He held out his hand and she shook it resentfully, her fingers sizzling when they brushed his as though he'd been wired up to the generator.

Not good, not good at all.

'Wow! Fancy bumping into you again, Libs.' Craig grinned. 'This is gonna be a blast.'

A blast was right. And he was fate-bound to be injured in the fallout.

'What are you doing here?' Libby hissed at Craig as they followed Eastwood through the set and towards the hotel. 'You said you were back-packing.'

'No, I didn't; you just assumed that,' Craig said reasonably. 'I never said anything about what I was doing.'

Oh. Actually that was right. But still, he had no right just turning up here where she worked! Having Craig around was going to make everything ten times more complicated, especially the staying away from men bit. It would be like going on a diet while locked in Willy Wonka's factory.

'You could have mentioned you worked in film,' she snapped.

He shrugged. 'I guess. But it never really seemed important. Besides,' he added, stopping in his tracks and placing a strong hand on her arm, 'I had other things on my mind.'

Libby stared up at him. 'Such as?'

He stepped in front of her and stopped. Libby swallowed. Craig's jade eyes sparkled as he reached out and brushed her hair back from her flushed cheeks. In spite of all her resolutions Libby felt a flame of desire.

'I can't possibly imagine, can you?' he murmured.

They were so close now that they were almost touching and her nipples beneath her flimsy cotton shirt couldn't have drawn more attention to themselves if they'd started glowing. He was just so sexy. She longed to slip her hands under the fabric of his T-shirt and feel the hard muscles of his chest, transported back for a minute to the deserted beach where they'd crash-landed and where his lips had found hers. At this memory her pulse went up a gear and in spite of this tsunami of desire she stepped away from him. God, she had to get a grip! This kind of reaction was exactly what she *didn't* want.

'Is having me here a problem?' Craig asked, looking hurt. 'I'd kind of hoped that it might be a nice surprise.'

'It is,' Libby said grudgingly. 'It's just that I'm not very good with surprises. Just ask my family, they'll tell you. Mum had a terrible time hiding presents from me when I was a kid. I couldn't rest until I'd found them all.'

'I can imagine you scaling the dizzy heights of the airing cupboard.' Craig grinned.

'It was the loft actually, and all hell broke loose when I put my foot through the plasterboard and into my sister's bedroom.'

Craig laughed and Libby couldn't help joining in. There was something about his good humour that made her heart rise like a helium balloon.

'I think we're going to have a lot of fun together,' Craig said and Libby felt her cheeks grow warm because the twinkle in his eyes suggested that he wasn't talking about work. As she drank in those toned abs and that bronzed skin she could imagine only too well the kind of fun he had in mind.

'Hey, you two, get your butts over here!' boomed Eastwood from the bar, and abruptly the spell was broken. Her pulse still racing, Libby smiled at Craig.

'We've been summoned.'

'I've only worked here for about five bloody minutes but already I figure we jump when he says,' Craig said.

'Yeah, and you ask how high – then double it!' Libby grimaced. 'He has everyone running about like R2-D2! You're in for a good time.'

Those bright eyes locked with hers again. 'I really, really hope so,' Craig said before striding off to join the hollering director. This left Libby staring after him, delicious goosebumps Mexican waving across her skin.

Oh, boy. This was going to be impossible.

As Craig spun and whirled, those strong muscular arms severing the air and powerful legs kicking past his ears before pounding into the sand, she felt her insides turn to a puddle of longing. He was so hot! From the flying blond curls and sleepy downturned eyes, to the powerful lean body and gigantic pecs, everything about him was raw sex appeal and she was shocked to find herself glued to his every move like a teenage girl at a Jonas Brothers concert!

It was early evening and Eastwood – a huge fan of martial arts and violence in general – had arranged for Craig to give a demonstration to the rest of the cast and crew on the set. Although he'd been fighting for nearly an hour he'd still managed to see off all his opponents. His skin was slick in the Thai heat but it was a good kind of slick, making his muscles gleam and moulding the fabric of his white lawn shirt to the lines of his body. Libby dragged her eyes away, feeling almost overwhelmed by how attracted to him she was.

Not that she was the only one who appreciated Craig's prowess. He'd attracted a large audience of crew, extras and cast alike. Even Trinity had lowered herself sufficiently to stroll over from her trailer to watch. After thirty minutes, her usually goldfish-like attention span hadn't wavered and she was watching Craig avidly. A small Thai woman stood by her side holding a parasol to shade her, easier said than done as every few minutes Trinity changed position.

'Shade me, quickly!' she was saying now, one red-nailed hand grabbing the handle of the parasol and yanking it so that her face was in shadow. 'Don't you understand how important my skin is?'

Personally Libby would have been tempted to wallop that same precious face with the carved ivory handle but fortunately for Trinity her companion was extremely professional and with a dip of her head and flick of a delicate wrist she managed to change the angle. Libby shook her head. Talk about vanity! If she hadn't been working with Trinity for the past few days Libby would have been inclined to think this was a continuity issue and that maybe the actress was susceptible to freckles, but she'd seen enough tantrums and diva-like outbursts to know better.

Trinity Duval was a nutter. And she was staring at Craig as though she wanted to gobble him up, which was pretty amazing in itself seeing as the woman seemed to exist on a diet of egg-white omelettes and fresh air. Talk about a cougar! Although she claimed to be twenty-nine, Libby was pretty certain you could add another ten years to that estimation and still be short of the truth, such were the wonders of Botox and lipo! As Craig finished with a high kick, Trinity was practically drooling. Who would have thought that a couple of flying *Kao Loi* kicks could knock all memory of Luke Scottman, Trinity's boyfriend, out of her head?

Maybe somebody should shoot this cougar with a tranquilliser dart, thought Libby drily. She looked ready to pounce at any minute. She turned her attention back to the makeshift arena where a hot and tired Craig was bringing his demonstration to a close. Poor guy. He'd only been working for Eastwood a few hours and already he looked ready to drop. After her gruelling day of casting, Libby totally sympathised. When slavery had been abolished somebody must have forgotten to tell Eastwood Jones.

'OK,' panted Craig, 'I think I've shown you all enough.' He raised his vest to mop his hot face and revealed a six-pack that would make He-Man jealous. 'Is there anything else you want to see?' Craig was asking the crowd as they clapped and cheered.

'More of that six pack!' somebody called and laughter rippled through the audience.

Craig grinned. 'How about I show you how this sport isn't all about strength. It's an ancient art of combat which allows even the lightest participant to take the advantage?'

The cheers died down a bit.

'A demonstration with one of us, you mean?' Eastwood said thoughtfully.

Craig nodded. 'I can show you that this is a battle of wits as much as physical strength. If you know the right techniques then, for once, size really doesn't matter.'

'It sounds wonderful,' Trinity cooed, hands fluttering to where her heart would be if she had one. 'I'd love to see you show us that. You're so enormously talented.'

Eugh! *Where's a sick bag when you needed one?* Libby thought with a grimace. Still, Craig wasn't to know just how horrendous Trinity really was, and like all men, he seemed to fall for the big blue eyes and candyfloss hair. Or should that be big boobs and candyfloss brain? Whatever, he was smiling at Trinity and asking for volunteers.

'I'd adore that!' Trinity was already scuttling towards him, the lethal rays of the sun totally forgotten in her excitement. But Eastwood Jones blocked her path swiftly and propelled her back to her parasol.

'You'll do no such thing!' he barked. 'You're the leading lady and you're far too delicate to hurl yourself around doing kung bloody fu! Besides, any bruises will be a pain in the butt for makeup.'

Trinity was about as delicate as a Sherman tank but there was no way she was going to argue with

Eastwood, not even to get her paws on Craig. Pouting, she settled back to her preening under the brolly. Craig looked relieved. As well he should. Trinity and her false nails were as lethal as any roundhouse.

'Someone else?' he asked. 'Preferably somebody who isn't vital to the entire movie though, just in case.'

'Me, Me! I fight you! I am warrior!'

Panom Yeerum leapt forward, jumping up and down as though on a pogo stick, and grinning from ear to ear like a Jack O' Lantern.

'O . . . K.' Craig looked seriously taken aback, as well he might. In spite of her earlier frustration with Panom, Libby started to giggle. What part of 'no' didn't the old dude understand? You really had to admire him; he didn't give up.

'Me, Me!' He was pleading now. 'Panom will help you. Panom can fight.'

Craig looked horrified. Fighting an elderly man wasn't quite what he'd had in mind, no matter how keen they were. Looking around at the crowd his gaze suddenly alighted on Libby and those green eyes locked with hers. Please, they said, *please!*

Libby pulled a wry face. Oh great, so it was like that, was it? Trinity was too precious to risk and Panom far too ancient but it was OK to bruise a lowly assistant casting agent. They were replaceable.

'Libby? Would you mind helping me?' Craig

stepped forward and beckoned to her while behind him Panom kept chanting, 'Me! Me! Me!' If he hadn't been asking her to make an exhibition of herself in front of the cast and crew Craig's predicament would have been quite funny.

'I do mind actually!' she hissed back. 'What makes you think I want to be thrown around like pizza dough?'

He laughed. 'Nice image! But I'd bet my last razoo you can hold your own.'

Libby didn't doubt this for a minute either. She was trained in martial arts, and was still fit and strong from all her sports and running. No, it was *him* she was worried about. Angela's warning was still ringing in her ears and besides she'd nearly killed Craig once already. This might only be a fun demonstration to him but who knew what might go wrong? She was just about to refuse when a yell from Eastwood to *get her butt over there now goddammit* left her with no choice but to do as she was told. What was it her birth chart had said? When fate calls loudly a Gemini leaps in. Who was she to argue with the stars?

'Thanks a bloody lot,' she grumbled when she joined Craig in the middle of his makeshift arena. 'I wish you *had* been a backpacker. I could really do without this.'

'Worried I might show you up, action woman?'

Craig teased. 'Or maybe you're afraid you won't be able to resist me if we get up close and personal for a second time?'

Libby swallowed. There was something in that. Craig was a vision of male gorgeousness and in a minute she'd have to let him touch her and place his hands on her bare skin.

'So, are you ready?' he wanted to know, advancing on her with a wide grin. He knew just how attracted to him she was, the absolute git! Instantly Libby's familiar competitive spirit kicked in. There was no way she was going to let him take advantage of that weakness. She might be physically smaller and slighter but she was strong and she was quick. Bring it on!

'Ready when you are,' she replied and her chin rose upwards in response to the challenge. 'Oh, by the way, I used to do a lot of tae kwon do when I was at uni.'

He raised his eyebrows. 'And you didn't think to mention this?'

'Sorry. It must have slipped my mind.'

'It's supposed to be a demonstration not a fight,' Craig pointed out mildly, but Libby screwed her nose up at this and seconds later they were engaged in a lightning fast dance across the sand. It didn't take her long to realise that she'd more than met her match. Good though she might be, he was brilliant, quick and smooth, moving lightly on the balls of his feet.

Oh, bollocks. She so had to get over this inability to resist a challenge!

'Come on, Libby,' Craig taunted. 'What's with the backing away? Take me down – if you can. I dare you!'

Argh! How come she'd only known this guy a few days and already he knew exactly how to press all her buttons? With lungs on fire Libby doubled her efforts, spinning and whirling like a dervish while her long blond hair whipped backwards and forwards across her cheeks. Once, twice, three times she tried to make contact with him but Craig was always out of reach, his fit body pinging away as though strung on elastic. Every lunge on Libby's part was met with thin air.

Spinning to the left she side-stepped him and whipped her right leg upwards aiming for his shoulder. It was supposed to be a killer move that in the past had won Libby several junior competitions but Craig was in another league altogether and within seconds she felt his arm rise to block her and instantly she was falling. Seconds later she was sprawled on the sand, her chest heaving and the sweat trickling between her shoulder blades while Craig loomed over her.

'I've got you, Libby,' he whispered, while she glowered up at him, too breathless from the fight to reply. At least she hoped it was the fight that was making her breathless. His face was so close to hers that their gasps mingled and she could see her reflection dancing in the inky blackness of his pupils. Time stood still for a split second as her heart fluttered against her ribcage and Craig held her captive beneath him.

Libby looked to the stars. If she really had a guardian angel, then now would be a good time to ask for some help. She was trying really hard to be a good girl here, easier said than done with a strong sexy guy between her thighs!

'You can't resist me forever,' Craig said with a wink.

Almost from nowhere she recalled some wrestling techniques she'd been taught years ago in a Fighting Fit class and, twisting her hips and pushing his shoulder in a move that totally took Craig by surprise, she flipped him over. Now it was Libby who was straddling Craig.

'As you see, size really doesn't matter,' she told him sweetly but Craig just laughed.

'You see?' He called over his shoulder to the on-lookers. 'Now she has the advantage.' Then, lowering his voice so that only she could hear, he added, 'Feel free to take advantage of me any time you like!'

While the crowd around them cheered and whistled, Libby dismounted with as much dignity as a girl who'd just been wrestled to the floor by an Aussie hunk possibly could. Leaving Craig still laughing she pushed her hair back from her hot face and, squaring her shoulders, walked to the bar and ordered herself a Diet Coke. With a double vodka thrown in just for good measure.

She had a horrible feeling that Craig was right. She wouldn't be able to resist him for much longer.

10

Exhausted after her exertions Libby slumped at the bar and sipped her drink. Out of the corner of her eye she watched Trinity wave Craig over and engage him in conversation. So the two of them were on pretty friendly terms already, were they? That hadn't taken long.

Oh, crap, now they were coming over to her. Or rather Craig was coming over and Trinity was following in his wake, her poor parasol girl trotting after her.

'Champagne,' she trilled, gesturing to the barman with a flap of her bejewelled hand. 'The best you have, obviously!'

Moments later, a condensation-streaked bottle of Cristal was nestling in an ice bucket while Eastwood and Trinity clutched brimming glasses of pale amber liquid and tried their hardest to persuade Craig to join them.

'Thanks, but no,' he told Trinity firmly, placing his hand over the top of the champagne flute. 'I never drink when I'm training. But maybe Libby would like a glass?'

Trinity would have curled her lip if it wasn't too stuffed with Botox to move. Suddenly horribly aware of the sweaty dirt-streaked contrast she must make to the immaculate actress, Libby muttered hastily that she was fine.

'Rubbish!' Craig said, sloshing champagne into the flute and passing it to her. 'You've earned a drink. There aren't many girls who can last that long against me. I'm impressed.'

He smiled at her and for a moment Libby basked in the warm sunshine of his admiration.

'Yes, yes,' interrupted Trinity, laying her hand on Craig's arm. 'But you were the star of the show. I was quite overcome watching you.'

Libby was quite overcome too . . . by the sudden need to puke! Accepting the drink anyway (after all, it wasn't every day she was offered Cristal) she sipped the sharp, biscuity liquid and tried to ignore her aching muscles.

'Have you worked on many films?' Trinity asked, batting heavily mascara'd eyes at him and peering up from under them like a Primark version of Princess Diana.

'You have no idea!' boomed Eastwood Jones, clapping Craig on the back. 'It's more a case of what he *hasn't* worked on! *Indiana Jones*, *Harry Potter* and the latest Bond film. Didn't you teach Daniel Craig the moves for the fight in the Monte Carlo hotel?'

Craig blushed. 'Aw, he didn't really need me.'

'I bet he did,' gushed Trinity. 'Dan's not as hard as everyone thinks he is.'

Libby doubted that Daniel Craig and Trinity Duval had ever met. But Trinity wasn't one to let a minor detail stop her. They were deep in conversation; Craig was recounting stories of his adventures and all the films he'd worked on while she chipped in with anecdotes about stars that she knew.

Trinity was all over him like a skinny blonde rash, asking questions she couldn't possibly be interested in hearing the answers to. Although with her rapt expression you'd have even thought she was fascinated by the finer points of managing the fight sequences for a low-budget art-house movie.

Turning down a second glass because she was starting to feel weary, Libby tried to ignore the sensation of Craig's eyes boring into her. It was probably in her imagination anyway. Why would he be staring at her when he had a Hollywood star drooling all over him?

Libby shook her head in frustration. Why did he have to show up now? It was going to make everything so complicated.

'Is this seat taken?'

Libby had been so lost in her thoughts she'd totally failed to notice that Dash Suri had strolled over. The childhood idol she'd daydreamed about for years was standing beside her and gesturing at the empty barstool. Libby flicked her hair back from her face, desperate to play it cool, but all she could hear was the Bhangra soundtrack playing and suddenly she was an awkward fourteen-year-old again. Any minute now and she'd be buying Guns N' Roses CDs and yelling that her mum didn't understand her.

'No, no! It's free. Please, sit down,' Libby gabbled, patting the seat. 'Nobody's sitting there.'

Oh, my God! Dash Suri was within touching distance! If only her teenage self could have known this moment would come.

'Cool. Thanks.' Dash slipped on to the stool, his feet dangling several inches short of the footrest, she noticed. Well, so what if he was a little bit vertically challenged? That was hardly a crime. He was still absolutely scrummy, all café au lait skin, razor sharp cheekbones and hair as dark and glossy as a raven's wing. He was well groomed, too, and beautifully dressed in a pure white dhoti embroidered with gold and crimson thread. Even his feet in their plain leather sandals looked as though they'd been buffed and manicured to within an inch of their lives. At least she'd had good taste when she was a teenager. How awful would that be, to discover that the guy you'd fantasised over all your formative years was really balding or had bad breath in real life?

It was a shame Dash was sitting next to Craig though. The Australian guy was so muscled and glowing with good health that in comparison Dash seemed a little bit . . . puny.

How could she have just thought that? This was Dash Suri! The man of her dreams.

'Hi, there. I'm Dash, Dash Suri,' Dash said, holding out a hand.

Libby shook it, hardly able to believe she was actually touching her hero. Goodness, but it was soft and smooth. Then Dash raised her knuckles to his mouth and brushed his lips against her hand and she started to feel mildly hysterical.

Deep breath, Libby! Play it cool. You don't fancy him any more, remember?

Feeling embarrassed about her own chewed nails and palms calloused from canoeing and climbing, she swiftly slipped out of the contact and tried to ignore her inner-teenager.

'And you are?' Dash asked, softly.

'I'm Libby,' she squeaked, sounding as though she'd been inhaling helium. Drat! That wasn't supposed to happen. She'd wanted to sound mature and confident, not like one of the Chipmunks. What must he think? But Dash was too busy checking his reflection in the ice bucket to really notice that Libby's face could double for a bottle of tomato ketchup.

'So, Libby, what do you do?' Dash wondered, once his hair was smoothed down and he was able to tear himself away from his reflection.

'Me? I'm just a casting assistant,' Libby said. 'A junior casting assistant. But I'm hoping to—'

'Have you ever seen any of my films?' Dash interrupted. 'I'm big in Bollywood, you know. *Mumbai Magic*? *Punjabi Princess*?'

Libby knew both of these off by heart and had the box sets of just about everything else he'd ever done. But weirdly, she didn't feel like discussing any of them. Dash might be beautiful but something about the way he was preening over her shoulder in the tinted hotel window reminded Libby of her granny's budgie. Any minute now he'd start tweeting and shouting, 'Pretty boy!' at the top of his lungs. Maybe she should call one of the waiters over and order some Trill?

This thought was so amusing that she tried to disguise her sudden giggles by taking a sip of Coke, which unfortunately she ended up snorting and spluttering everywhere. Eyes watering, Libby gasped for breath.

'Don't be embarrassed; I have this effect on quite a

lot of people,' he told her kindly. 'I can see you're overcome.'

'Oh, I am!' Libby wheezed. And she so was. Overcome by how vain her hero was, that was, as opposed to being bowled over by being this close to Dash at long last.

Weird. Perhaps she'd just grown out of him?

'You all right, Lib?' Craig called, looking concerned. 'Do you need me to come and give you some mouth to mouth?'

He did one of those searching emerald gazes into her eyes and Libby felt her cheeks grow hot. He was so annoying!

'She's just a bit starstruck,' Dash replied, tapping her ineffectively between the shoulder blades. It was a bit like being patted with a feather and Libby decided she was pretty lucky not to actually be choking. Dash might have played a doctor in umpteen films but in real life he hadn't got a clue.

'Jeez, that's some crush, mate,' Craig said slowly, his mouth twitching upwards with amusement. 'She can hardly breathe. Wish I had that effect on women. Libby just tries to kill me.'

He was laughing at her. He really thought she was all dreamy over Dash! Once her eyes had stopped streaming she sneaked a glance back at Craig, but he had his back to her and was laughing heartily at something Trinity had said. Libby tossed her hair in annoyance. Well, let him think that if he wanted. Dash was good-looking, but in a weirdly unsexy way, and he was pushing forty, for heaven's sake. Any attraction she'd first felt when meeting him was purely down to nostalgia.

'That was an impressive display you put on for us earlier,' Eastwood told Craig warmly. 'I knew you were good, but hell, that was something else.'

Craig shrugged. 'Thanks, but it's just my job.'

'You do it so well,' purred Trinity, running a red-tipped finger down his bicep. 'It must be because you're so strong.'

She was practically licking her lips and Libby thought that if Craig wasn't careful he'd be gobbled up before you could say *Aussie beefcake*! The same thought obviously crossed Craig's mind too because he gently removed her hand and said, 'That's what I'm here for; putting fight scenes together.'

Trinity pouted. 'There's more to life than work, you know.'

Libby agreed with her: some people had loves in their lives. And Trinity was supposed to love Luke Scottman!

'There's no time for anything but work on this set,' warned Eastwood Jones. 'We've only got a two-week window to shoot these scenes.' He put his empty beer glass down with a thud. 'In fact, I think we should get planning those scenes as soon as possible. Craig, you can join Trin, Dash and me for a run-through of the temple fight this evening.'

Dash lit up like Oxford Street in December. 'Fantastic! I can't wait. It'll be great for us to spend some time together on this. Seriously, Eastwood, I can't tell you how excited I am about filming the fights.'

Libby grimaced. Dash was practically drooling, obviously another fully signed-up member of the Trinity Duval fan club. Give guys a pair of baby-blue eyes, Jordanesque boobs and mane of blond hair and they practically rolled over and begged. Pathetic. And what a disappointment that Dash Suri was just as predictable. Talk about feet of clay – she could have made an entire dinner service out of his!

But Eastwood Jones wasn't listening to Dash. Instead he was studying a script, his brow creasing into a frown when he looked up.

'You! Lizzie!' he barked. 'You cast the fight scene so you'd better come too.'

'Libby,' Libby muttered, but Eastwood wasn't bothered about such minor details as a lowly casting assistant's name.

'Libby, Lizzie, call yourself Minnie Mouse for all I care! Just make sure you're in the bar at eight.'

'Can't wait!' Libby said, forcing a smile on to her lips. There went her evening swim.

'It'll be great to have you along,' said Craig warmly. 'You were fantastic on the beach earlier.'

Trinity threw her a look that could have curdled milk. Uh oh, thought Libby with a sinking heart. The older woman clearly had her sights set on Craig and wouldn't take kindly to anyone else attracting his attention. Although she had no intentions of anything happening with Craig, Libby had worked with enough self-absorbed and insecure leading ladies to know how difficult they could make things. With Tom AWOL, and Kyle and Janine avoiding her like the plague, things were already difficult enough without Trinity having it in for her.

'I need to get changed for dinner,' Trinity said to nobody in particular. Then she shot Libby an evil stare. 'Some of us prefer not to be sweaty and grubby. Do you want to come with me, Craig? You're more than welcome to use my trailer, and my personal chef is bound to have rustled up something simply delicious.'

Her smile was so sickly sweet that it was a miracle her Persil-white veneers didn't rot away, but Craig shook his head, those blond curls bouncing like springs.

'I'm fine, thanks. I'm going to dive in the ocean

then grab a bite with the crew. I need to catch up with Libs, too.'

He did? Libby was taken aback. Had Craig just turned down Trinity Duval or hadn't he realised that when she'd invited him for dinner that she was going to dish herself up as the main course?

'I'll catch you later, Trin,' he said chirpily before turning back to Libby.

'I'll hold you to that,' she purred, sashaying off with a toss of her mane.

'She will, too,' Eastwood said, once Trinity and her umbrella-bearing lackey were out of earshot. 'You'd better watch out, son!'

Craig grinned. 'Nice lady but definitely not my type. I like my women far more natural.' Then turning to Libby he added softly, 'And preferably jumping out of planes.'

Libby blushed. She simply couldn't help it. Normally she would have made a witty comment back or slipped away with him, but these weren't normal times. For one thing she was trying her hardest to prove that she was a mature professional casting agent – something which wouldn't exactly be proven by pulling the hunky martial arts instructor – and for another she was going to follow Angela's advice and give all men a wide berth. She'd already nearly got Craig killed, for heaven's sake! How much more of a warning did a girl need?

But if it hadn't been for that flipping prophecy she would have been sorely tempted . . .

Ignoring every yearning cell of her body, Libby slipped from her barstool and stepped away from him. 'I've got to go,' she said, a tsunami of blood sweeping into her face.

'Have you?' Craig fixed her with such a look of longing and desire that she almost faltered.

Torn, she nodded. 'I've got to find my boss. I'll catch you later.'

And then she was hurrying away from him with her heart racing and feeling horribly out of control. God, he was sexy. What a wicked waste!

Dash Suri *who*?

Working with Craig was going to be far more tricky than she'd thought . . .

Still horribly flustered, Libby headed back to her hotel room as fast as she could without actually breaking into a sprint and running. Where was a cold shower when a girl needed one? Honestly, what was she thinking, getting herself into such a state? It must be a combination of the oppressive heat and the champagne.

Well, the champagne and that lean, sexy muscular body.

She rested her forehead against the cool teak of her bedroom door and sighed. The shoot was only for two weeks. Surely she could keep her attraction to Craig under control for that long?

Inside, her room was blissfully chilly. Unseen hands had closed the blinds to shut out the blast-furnace sunshine and the ceiling fan whirred high above sending a cool breeze rippling across her skin. Libby flung herself backwards on to the bed, sending frangipani petals fluttering to the floor, and closed her eyes. The cotton sheets were crisp and cool and turning her head she pressed her hot cheek against the pillow.

Libby suddenly became aware that a low groaning sound was coming from the room next door. Sitting up and straining her ears, she could hear low and piteous moaning through the thin wall. The sound was intermittent, and sometimes drowned by the clicking of the fan or the burr of the air conditioning but it was definitely coming from the room next to hers.

Somebody was in agony.

Padding to the door that linked her suite to the one next to it, she pressed her ear up close, wincing in sympathy with each agonised whimper. Oh, Lord. She couldn't ignore that; whoever it was needed help.

'Hello?' She rapped her knuckles against the door. 'Are you OK?'

There was a brief pause before a weak voice croaked, 'Libby? Is that you?'

'Tom?' Libby was stunned. Tom had booked the room next door to hers, even though he'd brought Hilary with him? Of all the bloody cheek! He'd thought he'd have his cake, eat it and have seconds. Never mind taking the biscuit, this took the entire McVitie's warehouse.

But enough of the mixed and highly calorific metaphors. No matter that her opinion of Tom was lower than the worms right now, he sounded like he was in a bad way.

'Are you in the throes of passion with Hilary?' Libby thought she'd check before she barged in and saw something she'd need a lobotomy to forget. 'You're making a right racket.'

But her only reply was yet another groan, the depth and agony of which would put Marley's ghost to shame. Unlocking the door from her side, Libby peered through into Tom's room. Sunlight smacked her right between the eyes and she saw straight away that the bed was rumpled but empty.

'Tom?' she called, stepping through. 'Tom? Where are you?'

There was another groan, and as her eyes adjusted to the brightness Libby realised that the sound was coming from the en-suite. Marching across the room she flung open the door and discovered Tom kneeling on the floor and clutching the toilet bowl as though his life depended upon it. For a second Libby was stunned. This wreck of a man wasn't the suave Tom she was used to. Gone were the designer shades, clean-shaven face and artfully styled hair. In their place was a shivering, hollow-cheeked figure with sweat-dampened hair and green-tinged skin.

'What's happened?' Libby gasped, dropping to her knees and pressing her hand against Tom's forehead. Pushing her away, he retched into the toilet bowl, great dry heaves that left him shaking and slumped against the porcelain.

'How on earth have you got yourself in this state?' Libby wondered aloud. They'd eaten the same food, taken care not to eat fruit or salad, had taken all the usual precautions necessary when travelling in the Far East. Then she recalled how he'd borrowed her hat earlier. 'Is it heat stroke?'

Tom clutched his stomach and retched again while Libby held his hair back from his face. Then she soaked a flannel in cold water and sponged his burning forehead. He might have been an utter shit to her but Libby couldn't bear to see anyone in distress. Not even cheating scumbag ex-boyfriends.

'Did you eat something bad?' she asked.

Slowly and painfully, Tom lifted his head and

nodded towards the bedside cabinet.

'It was that,' he croaked, pointing at an empty bottle of water.

Libby gulped. Surely that wasn't . . .

'The water you gave me earlier,' Tom croaked piteously. 'It must have been filled from a local tap.'

There was another ominous rumble from his tummy that, unless Tom was related to Vesuvius, was her cue to leave the bathroom very fast. Swiftly backing out, Libby left him to his misery. Picking up the empty bottle, Libby quickly realised that although the label had been genuine the seal had probably already been broken when she'd purchased it. She'd been in far too much of a rush to check when she'd bought it and Tom had probably just assumed that she'd already had a sip.

A few minutes later Tom staggered into the bedroom looking even worse if anything. His skin was greener than seaweed and he was trembling like a puppy left out in the rain. If he hadn't been such a cheating git Libby would almost have felt sorry for him.

'How come you're OK?' he groaned.

'I never drank any,' Libby confessed. Closing her eyes she saw again the sweet face of the little Thai girl who'd been selling her wares by the lapping waves. She'd not touched her fruit – guessing that it had probably been washed in untreated water – but she'd assumed the drink would be safe. If only she'd thought to check the seal. 'I'm so sorry.'

But Tom was beyond listening to apologies. With a pitiful wail he'd torn back to the bathroom where he was retching and groaning again.

Libby exhaled slowly. Where was bloody Hilary when you needed her? Annoyed as she was with Tom there was no way she could leave him in this state. He'd be dangerously dehydrated and needed looking after. Judging by the sounds that were coming from the en-suite she really ought to call a doctor.

One thing, though, that she did know for sure was that Angela's prophecy was one hundred per cent accurate. She'd have to be really careful from now on.

Much later, and after much brow-mopping and swallowing of electrolytes, Libby finally managed to get a very poorly Tom off to sleep. The doctor had visited and diagnosed a really nasty case of gastroenteritis and given strict instructions that Tom did nothing but rest for at least five days. Which was fair enough, Libby thought, bearing in mind just how unwell he was, but it really left her in at the deep end with regards to the casting for the film. Hilary still hadn't shown up even though Libby had sent her several texts to say that Tom was ill. It seemed she'd vanished in a puff of Chanel-scented smoke and had no intention of reappearing any time soon.

Closing Tom's bedroom door with a soft click, Libby decided that she didn't blame Hilary for not wanting to be near him after what he'd done, but her disappearing act had certainly dropped the rest of the team in it. With Tom now out of action and no sign of Hilly, it was down to Libby and Kyle to take charge of the casting. Which was easier said than done seeing as Kyle was still avoiding her.

Down in the lobby, all was quiet. Glancing at her ancient Snoopy watch, Libby saw it was a lot later than she'd thought. Dinner was long over and the majority of guests were either in the bars or headed into the nearest town. Missing supper wasn't really a problem: after spending hours cleaning up after Tom, Libby didn't think she could face eating anyway, but she could certainly do with a drink.

Shit! Libby's hands flew to her mouth. She'd been summoned to drinks with Eastwood, hadn't she? But in the midst of the vomiting trauma this had totally slipped her mind. Great, that was going to be a big black mark in her copybook. It was too late now though; she'd just have to apologise later and explain what had happened. She'd do this tomorrow; she didn't fancy joining the party this late and, anyway, in contrast to the immaculate Trinity she'd look like a grubby wreck. And she probably didn't smell too great either . . .

Pausing by an enormous potted palm, Libby took a moment to contemplate her next move. Hmm. Should she try knocking on Kyle and Janine's door, risking the outbreak of World War Three, or should she just grab a Diet Coke and chill out by the sea for a bit? The thought of sinking into soft, warm sand, growing dizzy as she peered up at the star-freckled sky was very appealing. She had her bikini on under her clothes so she could even have a quick swim.

Yes, that seemed like a plan. But just as she was about to leave the shelter of the potted palm, the shrill notes of Trinity's laughter scraped the air. Peeking through the green fronds Libby saw Eastwood, Craig and Trinity stroll into the lobby. She'd better stay put for a minute: there was no point drawing attention to the fact she'd missed their meeting.

'Right, kids, I'm hitting the hay. Early start for us tomorrow so you should do the same,' Eastwood was saying, slapping Craig on the back. It was a testament to the Aussie guy's strength that he didn't topple like a felled tree.

Trinity pouted, looking like a blonde puffer fish. 'But, honey, it's so early!'

'And we're shooting at sunrise,' the director said firmly. 'I'll catch you guys tomorrow.'

Left alone, Trin turned to Craig and rising on to tiptoes whispered into his ear. Craig tipped his head back and laughed his infectious velvety laugh. Then a loud ping announced the arrival of the lift, the doors hissed open and Craig followed Trin inside, one strong tanned hand placed firmly in the small of her back. Seconds later they were gone, sailing upwards until it reached the top floor where the stars were staying in luxury ocean-view suites and Libby didn't need psychic skills to tell her where they were going and why.

So much for Craig preferring natural women!

Seeing Craig and Trinity together was like getting a sucker punch to the guts. Although she had no intentions of getting involved with Craig – she liked the guy and wanted him to live, after all – it was still pretty galling to see him taken in by someone like Trinity Duval. The woman was shallower than a flea's paddling pool!

She'd only just stepped out of her hiding place when the sight of Kyle and Janine heading through the lobby towards the bar sent her back behind her palm. They were deep in conversation, crisis talks by the look of it, and the last thing they needed was her popping up to spoil things. Blast! They were coming in her direction now and without some serious camouflage gear and SAS-style stripes across her face there was no way they'd miss her. To her left was a door marked 'function room' and as quietly as she could Libby pushed it open and slipped inside.

The room was dark and for a second she couldn't see anything. As her eyes adjusted to the gloom, Libby noticed that rather than the chairs and tables she'd expected, the room was draped from ceiling to floor with swathes of muslin which drifted like a soft rainbow and whispered with every click of the whirring fan.

Weird. Why would anyone deck out a perfectly good function room to look like the inside of a sheik's tent? Was this part of the set? Perhaps the very spot where Trinity, all golden skin and flimsy harem gear, would recline on plump cushions and seduce Craig? Err – Dash. Err – the Indian Prince, she meant!

It was a strange place for shooting, though, thought Libby as she pushed her way through the muslin tangles. Far too near the lobby and the clatter of the kitchens to allow for clean takes, she'd have guessed. Besides, she'd not seen any mention of this room on her location list and shooting schedule.

As her eyes adjusted to the dim light, Libby saw that she wasn't alone. Silhouetted through the final drapes were two figures. Pushing gently through the fabric she saw a man and a woman on either side of a table, which was covered in tarot cards. Ah! So this was a set of a kind! The room had been dressed like a tent and set aside for psychic readings. Casting her mind back to when they'd first arrived at the hotel, Libby thought she remembered Janine telling her that the hotel had a resident fortune-teller. Maybe she should have paid a visit? It could have saved a whole heap of trouble.

'But what can I do?' she heard a man say. 'It's

torture for me, being this close but not being able to say how I really feel!' Through the gauze she could see his head was in his hands and he had his back to her, but Libby would have known that voice anywhere. She ought to, seeing as she'd spent the majority of her formative years listening to it.

'Can you imagine what it's like for me?' Dash continued, shaking his glossy head despairingly. 'It's all I can think about, all I long for, and it's just so totally and utterly impossible.'

'Does your love know of your feelings?'

'No idea. It's killing me. I have to speak my mind!'

'Be careful about revealing your feelings too soon,' warned the psychic. 'The cards say that you must bide your time.'

Dash groaned. 'I can't. We might never be together like this again! We work on such different films. This could be the only chance I have.'

Libby was instantly intrigued. So, Dash was secretly in love with somebody he worked with? While the psychic concluded the reading she struggled to figure out who the mystery person could be, puzzling over this as though playing romantic sudoku. It was probably Trinity, she decided finally with a mental eye roll. Men seemed to go all gooey over those big eyes, breathless cute voice and fluffy dandelion-clock hair, which was ironic really, seeing as Trin was actually as fluffy as a tyrannosaurus rex. Libby didn't need the psychic to predict that poor Dash was in for a broken heart. Especially seeing as at this exact minute Trin was doing her bit for American–Aussie relations. Not to mention the fact that she was in a relationship with Luke Scottman.

Once Dash had left the room, still muttering about declaring his feelings come what may, Libby pushed through the final swathe of curtains. She felt bad about overhearing his reading, however accidentally. His secret was safe with her though. Libby was scatty and reckless but she wasn't a gossip.

'You want a reading?' the psychic asked, catching sight of her. A small Thai woman with a face as wrinkled as a raisin, she swept bright dark eyes over Libby and tutted loudly. 'You *need* a reading. You sit.'

Something about the certainty in her voice stopped Libby in her tracks. It was the same assured tone that Angela had used, a confidence that she was imparting knowledge that only she had the ability to access, and Libby sat down. She could certainly do with some cosmic input. Phoning dial-a-psychic from Thailand was a much more expensive option.

'Cross my palm with silver,' said the psychic. 'Or I take Amex.'

Libby smiled. 'How about I give you my room number and you charge to that?'

The woman nodded and, taking Libby's door card, scribbled down the details. *Maybe I should have asked how much she charges*, Libby thought. But it was too late now because she was shuffling the cards and cutting them just like she had with Angela. Then the old woman was laying them out in an elaborate pattern.

'You have a man in your life,' she said.

Libby laughed a hollow laugh. 'Not any more.'

'You angry with this man. You not happy with him.'

That is the understatement of the year, Libby thought.

The woman wagged a bony finger. 'You need be careful in Thailand. You must not tie you self up in knots.'

Libby started as though scalded. 'What? What did you say?'

'Be careful. Not get tied up in knots,' the psychic repeated. 'Is a message from the spirits to you.'

Libby felt goosebumps ripple across her body. After what had happened with the parachute jump it was surely too spookily close to the truth to be a coincidence? Feeling chilled to the bone she couldn't help thinking there had to be something in it. Being a danger to men and having to take care in Thailand seemed to be far too similar for comfort. She had to listen to these messages.

Even when the psychic went on to charge her $300 for the reading, Libby couldn't help thinking it was money well spent. After all, she'd nearly killed Craig and almost poisoned Tom. If she didn't heed these cosmic warnings something serious was sure to happen.

12

Heading back into the lobby Libby saw Kyle and Janine standing hand in hand by the lifts. Hey, that looked hopeful. Could they be making up?

She was just debating whether or not to join them when a tall blond man swept around the corner from reception, causing a ripple of excitement to spread through the onlooking guests. All eyes in the place were on him but the man seemed oblivious as he laughed away. Dash Suri was scuttling in his wake, laughing too. Libby's jaw dropped. Could it really be him? Could Luke Scottman – A-list celebrity and her sister's friend from university – really be here in Thailand?

It was definitely him! A more polished and gym-honed version, it was true, but that good-natured laugh was just the same as it had always been. In fact, just hearing it was enough to bring her back to those days when she was dazzled by Zoe's exciting friends and university freedoms. Luke had been a part of her sister's set and had dated Zoe's friend Fern for years. Libby's crush on Dash had been at its height during this time, and no matter how gorgeous Luke was, he'd never had a look-in. Instead he'd been more like an annoying big brother, tweaking her pony tail and teasing her about being skinny. Now he was one half of the most talked about celebrity couple on the planet. Did she dare say hello?

Of course she did. He was still Luke, and after the traumas of the last few days it was brilliant to see a familiar face, even if it was one she was more used to seeing on billboards or the big screen.

'Hey!' Libby yelled across the lobby. 'Spotty Scottie!'

Luke Scottman swung round, his face splitting into a wide and dazzling white smile when he caught sight of her. *Wow*, thought Libby, taken aback by the perfect teeth. Those were definitely a new addition since the uni days!

'Oh my God!' Luke was hollering, striding over to pick her up and twirl her around. 'It's Lanky Libby! And she's not much of a string bean any more! What the hell are you doing here?'

'I'm working,' Libby told him when he finally released her from a bear hug. 'I'm a casting agent.'

'Wow, that's great!' Luke said warmly, his sparkling blue eyes twinkling down at her. 'But I'm confused. I thought you were going to be a professional parkour athlete?'

Libby blushed. She'd forgotten about that stage. She'd driven everyone mad for months, and goodness knows how she hadn't broken her neck with all the tree climbing and jumping off walls. Luke and Zoe had even had to prize her down from Nelson's column on one occasion.

'Hey, I'm teasing!' Luke ruffled her hair with a strong and well-manicured hand. 'It's great you're in casting. I bet your bosses couldn't do without you!'

'Hmm,' said Libby, thinking about Tom, who was now best friends with the en-suite loo and probably at this very moment planning how he could sack her. Still, there was no point going into all this right now. Swiftly changing the subject, she asked, 'How come you're here? You're not in this film are you?'

'God, no!' shuddered Luke. 'Not my thing at all, all that mincing round in robes and singing! Sorry, Dash, no offence, but give me a good old action movie any day.'

'No, no,' Dash said quickly. 'I totally agree. I'd far rather do an action film than a musical.'

He would? Libby couldn't have been more surprised if Dash had told them he was a bin man in his spare time. Gorgeous though he was, a less likely start of an action movie it would be hard to imagine:

this Bollywood dreamboat was more boy band than blockbuster. In her opinion Bruce Willis had nothing to worry about.

'I've been shooting a cameo up country so I decided I'd pop down and visit Trin,' Luke explained. 'We haven't seen each other for a few weeks so I thought I'd surprise her.'

Shit, thought Libby. He'd do that all right if he discovered Trin and Craig together. She didn't like Trinity much but Luke was a nice guy and didn't deserve to walk in on that!

'Why don't we have a quick drink first?' she suggested, tucking her hand into the crook of his arm. 'It's been ages since I last saw you and we've got loads of catching up to do. I can tell you all about Zoe's wedding too.'

Luke looked pleased at this suggestion. 'Hey, why not? But only lemonade for you, young lady!'

In a very mature fashion Libby poked her tongue out. 'I'm twenty-four now!'

Complaining that she was making him feel ancient, Luke invited Libby to join him and Dash in the VIP area. Libby tried to act cool but she couldn't help staring at the plush interior, all ornate gold paint and red velvet sofas. She didn't see anyone famous, unless you counted Luke and Dash, of course, but she did notice lots of stunningly beautiful women with the caramel-streaked hair and the glossy look of the uber-rich. She noticed all of them staring at her; or, more accurately, staring at her and probably wondering what on earth Luke Scottman was doing with such a scruffy urchin.

As mobile-phone cameras flashed and people whispered behind their champagne glasses Libby was struck by the realisation that she wasn't with Spotty Scottie any more but one of Hollywood's most lusted after stars. Maybe the guy who'd once loved to sink cheap lager and guzzle the greasiest doner kebab possible was still there beneath the groomed and fit exterior, but there were only a few people on the surface of the planet who knew that man. To the rest of the world he was Luke Scottman: A-lister, subject of a million female fantasies and hotter than the nuclear core of Sellafield.

She wondered if he could still belch *God Save the Queen*? Never mind the acting stuff, *that* was a real talent!

They sat in a private booth, away from the scorching stares of the other guests, and Luke ordered a bottle of Krug as casually as though it were cheap plonk. When it came to fine wines her knowledge had more holes than Swiss cheese. She was lucky to afford a bottle of cava and that was only on pay day. So she nearly choked on her drink when Dash pointed out that the bottle had just cost Luke in excess of seven hundred dollars.

'Bloody hell, Luke,' Libby spluttered. 'That's a ridiculous amount of money to spend on booze!'

'Says the girl who used to spend all her student loan on cider!' Luke grinned. 'Relax, Libs, I'm a movie star now, remember? People expect me to spend bloody stupid amounts on champagne. If I *don't* then they start to get worried. Believe me I'd rather have a Bud!'

Dash shuddered. 'How can you prefer beer to vintage Krug?'

'Because I'm just a pleb at heart?' Luke suggested with a wink.

Libby sipped her drink. It break-danced on her tongue, crisp and glacial and was utterly delicious but she couldn't help but think what a dent the price of the bottle would have made in her credit card bill. She must be a pleb as well.

'So, any truth in this rumour I hear that you're in line to be the next Bond?' Dash asked Luke.

Luke pulled a face. 'If I had a quid for every time I get asked that!'

'Nice try, Luke, but I need an answer,' Dash pressed. One hand toyed with his champagne glass, long slender fingers tapping incessantly against the crystal. Hmm, not as relaxed as he looked then, Libby noted with interest. Why was he so interested in what films Luke was in and his movements for the next few months? Was he after the Bond role?

'I don't have one, I'm afraid,' Luke said firmly. 'But if they ever need a captain for the starship *Enterprise* then I'm there!'

Libby groaned. 'Oh Lord spare us. You'll not still a sad Trekkie are you?'

'Trekker!' admonished Luke.

'He was always mad on *Star Trek*,' Libby explained to the bemused Dash. 'One year, he and Fern even threw a party where everyone had to come dressed as characters from the show. I think my sister still has the pictures somewhere. Maybe I should offer them to the *Sun*? I can see the headlines now! *Luke Scottman's Klingon fetish!*'

'Watch it, Lanky! Or some of those embarrassing brace photos might get into the wrong hands,' Luke warned.

She held up her hands. 'OK, OK! You've got me there!'

'They were good times though, weren't they?' he said. 'Sometimes I think they were the best of my life; I just didn't realise it then.'

Dash nodded his glossy dark head. 'Youth is certainly wasted on the young.'

'God, will you two just listen to yourselves!' Libby couldn't believe her ears. 'You're both successful, rich and mega famous. What on earth is there to be nostalgic about? Luke, you have a Hollywood mansion. Surely you can't miss that minging student flat? There were slugs in the kitchen and I don't think anyone ever cleaned the bathroom except Zoe!'

An emotion flickered across Luke's face. It looked almost like regret but it was gone so quickly and it was dark in the bar too, so she must have been mistaken. What on earth could Luke have to regret?

'Is your sister still blazing a trail of glory at the Beeb?' he asked.

Libby laughed. 'Something like that. She's just finished another costume drama, I think. A Henry James adaptation, or something. She was revising like mad when I left.'

'Libby's sister works in TV,' Luke told Dash, who looked so at sea it was amazing he wasn't sitting in a boat. 'She's done loads, including that really raunchy modern *Jane Eyre*.'

'The one with Clive Owen in wet shirt and trousers?' Dash said, perking up. 'I caught that when I was in Mumbai. It was excellent.'

Libby was touched by his enthusiasm. She was pretty keen on the Clive Owen bit herself.

'Zoe got a Bafta for that. It's got pride of place in the loo.'

'That sounds like the modest Zoe I know,' Luke

said warmly. 'How is she, by the way? Happily married?'

'Very.' Libby fished her phone out of her pocket, scrolled through to the pictures section and passed it to him. Luke flipped through the pictures, his chiselled face inscrutable while Dash peered over his shoulder.

'She looks beautiful,' he said finally. 'And that skinny bird in the pink dress didn't scrub up too badly either.'

'Cheeky!' Libby reclaimed her phone.

'I never knew you had legs. Did they have to surgically remove your tracksuit bottoms?'

She punched him on the arm. Ow! That was solid muscle these days.

'I'm all grown up now, Pukey Lukey. Besides, people change, you know.'

He sighed. 'They sure do. And I've changed because I'm shattered. Gone are the days when I could stay up all night chatting. I think it's time I turned in.'

'So soon?' Dash's liquid eyes filled with disappointment. 'We've only just got started.'

'You guys carry on. I need to go and find Trin. She'll go nuts if she finds out I've been down here rather than popping up to find her.'

Libby's pulse accelerated so quickly that she had to clutch the bar table for support. There was no way Luke could go up to the penthouse suite and find Trinity and Craig together. She'd be a danger to two men if she let that happen! She could see the headlines already, floating past her eyes like the tabloid equivalent of Macbeth's dagger. *Film Star hurls Aussie from Balcony! Luke Scottman injured in bedroom brawl!*

She'd seen enough of Angela's warnings come true already to risk ignoring this one. She'd never forgive herself if something awful happened and she'd done nothing to try and stop it.

'Don't go upstairs!' she cried.

Dash and Luke stared at her. Oops. That had come out rather more loudly than she'd anticipated. Taking a deep breath and making a conscious effort to lower her voice by a few decibels she added, 'I mean there's no point going upstairs because Trinity isn't there.'

Luke raised an eyebrow so expertly that it was amazing the James Bond team didn't sign him on the spot.

'Really? So where's Trin then?'

'She's in her trailer,' Libby improvised wildly. 'I saw her heading that way earlier on. She said she was going to rehearse her lines with someone.'

Luke looked taken aback. 'Blimey, that's not like Trin. She normally leaves everything to the last minute. Either the heat's got to her, or she's actually taking this film seriously!'

'Then she's the only one,' Dash said gloomily, sloshing more champagne into his glass. 'I mean, have you read the script?'

Luke grimaced. 'Unfortunately for me, when Trin was going for the role I was made to read your bits more times than I care to remember. The military should adopt it as a form of torture.'

'Is it that bad?' Libby asked, pleased to be buying some time with this discussion.

Dash fixed her with big sad eyes. 'Put it this way; when the time comes for nominations for the Palme d'Or I don't think Spielberg will be losing any sleep!'

'It's pure cheese,' Luke confirmed cheerfully. 'Never mind,' he added, clapping Dash on the shoulder. 'People love that stuff. It'll probably make millions.'

And leaving Dash to ponder this happy thought he bid them both goodnight and strode out of the bar, totally oblivious to the longing glances that burned into his back.

Libby turned to say goodbye to Dash too. Now that Luke had left it was as though the sun had slipped behind a cloud; there'd be no way the Bollywood idol would want to sit and chat to a nobody like her. Yet to her surprise Dash showed no signs of moving but had settled back into his plush seat and was swirling his drink thoughtfully.

'So, Libby,' he said in that deliciously accented voice, 'unless I am very much mistaken I think I saw you leave the psychic's suite earlier. Yes?'

Libby's blood turned to ice water. Oh, bollocks! Had he seen her lurking behind the curtains? Was he about to tear a strip off her for eavesdropping?

But Dash didn't look very angry; in fact, he gave her a smile of such sweetness that her heart did a little roly poly. He still had the old magic.

'What did you make of her?' he continued. 'Do you think she was accurate?'

Libby was torn. Part of her wanted nothing more than to stay and chat to him but the other part of her was already stressing about how long it would be before Luke found that Trin wasn't in her trailer and went charging up to the suite. Should she race up there to warn Craig? She supposed she ought to but the mental image of his golden body entwined with Trin's tango orange one made her feel quite queasy.

'I thought she was good,' she told him quickly. 'She knew things about me that I've not shared with anyone else.'

Dash sat bold upright, sloshing champagne all over the table. 'It was exactly like that for me, too! She knew everything! Secrets I have never shared with another soul.' He leaned forward and dropped his voice in a confidential tone. 'She told me I have to be honest about my feelings for someone and not keep them secret for a minute longer.'

'Wow!' Libby was impressed. 'That's pretty specific.'

'I thought so too. So she must be right, mustn't she? I need to go and tell this person how I feel!'

Out of the corner of her eye Libby glimpsed the gilt clock. Seven minutes had passed since Luke had gone off in search of Trinity. Surely that was more than enough time for a potential James Bond to reach his girlfriend's trailer and realise she wasn't there? Would he come back to the bar or just head straight up to her room?

Oh, crap! What if he'd already done that?

'Libby? Should I?' Dash laid one smooth hand on her arm. 'Do you think I should?'

Did she think he should what? Libby stared at him, before nodding enthusiastically. If she agreed with him then maybe they could end this conversation and she could still stop Luke from discovering what his beloved really got up to on set!

'Hmmm. I'm sure she's right,' she said.

Dash squared his shoulders. 'If you think it's a good idea then it's exactly what I must do! I have left it far too long.' His eyes shone with the zeal of a religious fanatic and as he jumped to his feet Dash clasped her hands and squeezed them tightly. 'Thank you, thank you.'

'It's no problem,' Libby laughed, slipping her hands free and sliding out of her seat. 'Glad I could help.'

'More than you'll ever know,' Dash said. 'Now, let me buy you another drink.'

She held her hands up. 'Thanks, but I've got a few things to do.'

Leaving Dash in the bar to finish his champagne, Libby shook her head. She could hardly believe she was walking away from her fantasy. Her teenaged self was shouting 'NO!' very, very loudly, but her twenty-four-year-old self knew that something had to be done about Craig and Trin.

Outside in the black velvet darkness, crickets chirruped and the air was swollen with the scents of lemongrass and hot earth. Libby raced through the lush hotel gardens and then across the car park towards the place where the trailers had been parked. Several crew members called to her as she tore past but Libby didn't have time to stop. Instead she just waved and continued on her way, weaving between the aisles of parked vans until she arrived at the pink monstrosity that was Trin's personal trailer.

Gasping, Libby paused by the door until her breath was less ragged. Closer investigation revealed that all was dark and silent. Trin's trailer was deserted and even as she hammered on the door Libby already knew there'd be no answer.

She must have missed Luke. Which meant he was probably already on his way to Trin's suite and certain disaster. Gulping in another lungful of air, Libby began to sprint back through the empty trailer lot. She had a stitch in her side but she gritted her teeth and ignored it. All that mattered was that she managed to stop Luke discovering Craig and Trin en flagrante.

There was just one last hope left, one final chance that Craig didn't have a fist-shaped dent in his face, which was that Luke might not know where Trin's trailer was and still be searching the lorry park. There was a Posh Spice-thin chance that he was still scanning the trailers.

'Luke?' Libby called, as she wove in and out of the Winnebagos. 'Luke?'

But the only reply was the echo of her voice and the distant whisper of the waves. This was a waste of time, she though bleakly as she sagged against the final trailer to catch her breath. What was plan B?

Bollocks. There was no plan B. It looked as though Angela's prophecy was going to come true after all. Not even Usain Bolt would be able to catch Luke up now. He was probably punching Craig at this very second.

So deep was Libby in these gloomy imaginings that when the door of the trailer she was leaning against flew open she jumped so high that she practically needed oxygen. Then strong arms had snaked around her body. Before she could even register what was happening, she was lifted upwards and pulled inside the trailer so fast that she didn't even have time to scream.

Libby was being abducted!

13

The trailer door slammed shut and she was plunged into the dark interior. For a split second her unknown assailant's grip loosened as he reached out to fasten the door, so seizing her moment Libby twisted violently to the left, causing him to stumble. She'd heard enough stories about young women being assaulted or worse out in the Far East and had absolutely no intention of becoming another statistic. Wrenching free her right arm she drove it backwards with all her might into the taut muscles of his stomach. There was a bellow of pain and then she was free, giddy with the fear and sudden rush of adrenalin. Before he could come after her again she flew for the door and frantically yanked at the handle. *Hurry!* she told herself frantically. *You have to get out before he gets his breath back!*

'Ow, Libby,' the doubled-up figure gasped from the gloom. 'That really hurt!'

Startled, Libby's hand dropped from the lock. She

knew that voice. Turning slowly and with her eyes rapidly adjusting to the darkness she saw that her attacker – still clutching his stomach and groaning – was none other than Luke Scottman.

'Jesus, Luke, you nearly scared me to death! What the hell are you playing at?'

Luke's face swam towards her through the half-light. 'Sorry, Libs, I didn't mean to make you jump.'

'Jump? I practically went to Mars and back!' Now that the shock was wearing off she felt weak with relief that she wasn't about to be gutted like a fish by a guy in a scream mask. She was also mightily pissed off with Luke for scaring her so badly. 'What were you thinking, grabbing me like that?'

Luke sighed heavily and raked a hand through his thick golden hair.

'You're going to think I'm mad, but I was trying to protect you.'

'By giving me a heart attack?' Libby goggled at him. Seriously, all that celebrity stuff must have gone to Luke's head. 'Tell me, what do you do to people you want to harm?'

Luke sighed heavily.

'I've got a stalker, or rather *we've* got a stalker. Me and Trin. He's addicted to the *Scinity* brand. He always seems to know where we're going to be staying or shooting and he sends us these crazy letters made up of letters snipped out of the magazines. Then he, he . . .' Luke paused. 'Then he . . .'

'Then he what?'

Luke swallowed. 'Then he superimposes our faces on to . . . erm, pornographic photos, and posts them to our management team.'

'Eugh!' Libby exclaimed. 'That's totally gross!'.

'Eugh indeed. And hardly the behaviour of a sane human being, I'm sure you'll agree.'

Libby did agree. Suddenly she was very glad indeed that she was just a humble casting agent rather than a world-famous movie star!

'Anyway,' Luke continued, 'lately the stuff this nutter sends has got weirder and weirder and our security team's told us we really need to be careful. He could be harmless, but on the other hand there are enough crazies out there to make us both a bit nervous. Mark David Chapman shot Lennon after all, and Gwyneth Paltrow's stalker got sectioned.'

'Can't you take a conjunction out or something?'

'An *in*junction?' He shook his head. 'Nice thought, but we've got no idea who this guy is. All we know is that he keeps close tabs on us. Wherever we are he won't be too far away.'

Libby followed his gaze over her head and through the window. Outside the moon had been smothered by cloud and the narrow aisles between the trailers were gloomy and shadowed. How easy would it be for an obsessed fan to lurk in the gloom and wait for Luke or Trin? She gulped. The answer was *far too easy*.

'After I left you I was waylaid outside the bar by a very weird fan,' Luke continued slowly. His eyes seemed to darken with worry and a muscle clenched in his smooth tanned cheek. 'I can't be sure whether this guy is the stalker or not but he was certainly really keen to have my autograph. Anyway, I signed his book and chatted a bit then I hurried away to find Trin. But this guy was following me.'

'Are you sure?'

Luke nodded. 'He kept his distance but he was there all right. I kept stopping and then he'd flatten himself against a trailer or duck behind one. It seriously freaked me out. So I decided to hide and wait it out here. When I saw you wandering past I was horrified. The last thing I wanted was for you to stumble across our deranged stalker. He might have thought you were meeting me for a secret tryst or something and that I'm cheating on Trin. Things like that push nutters over the edge, you know.'

'But you and Trin would never cheat on each other! Everyone knows that,' Libby said, a little too hurriedly. 'But, I forgive you for scaring the crap out of me.'

Luke smiled, but it didn't quite meet his eyes and for the first time Libby noticed the lines of strain that traced each side of his mouth. She was just about to try and make a joke to lighten the mood when the door handle moved up and down violently before the entire door was rattled.

Libby froze and Luke paled beneath the tan. Pressing his finger against his lips they watched as the handle jerked upwards and downwards twice more. Libby's mouth dried with fear. Way to go, she told herself, this is all your fault! If it weren't for her, Luke would be safely inside the hotel with hot and cold running security guards, rather than stranded in an isolated Winnebago with a deranged stalker waiting outside. Heaven knew what a crazed fan would do when he captured one half of his idealised couple in close quarters with another woman.

The prophecy was about to strike again. Danger to men? She ought to come with a government health warning!

Holding their breath and not daring to move so much as an eyelash, Libby and Luke waited the rattling out. Finally the handle slowly returned to its original position and they heard footsteps walking away from them. For a few minutes they kept still and silent, hardly daring to exhale, until they could no longer hear anything.

'Jeez,' Luke whispered, one hand held over his heart. 'I think I just lost about ten years of my life. I had visions of being stuffed in a boot or something like the girl in that Emimen video.'

Libby said. 'That one about the crazy fan. Please tell me that the guy you bumped into didn't have a chainsaw and a Hannibal Lecter mask?'

'Hardly. He was just some old Thai dude. Kept coming out with the most bizarre things. He sounded like a talking fortune cookie.'

Libby felt laughter building up inside her like a geyser. This all sounded reassuringly familiar. She suddenly realised that they weren't being stalked by a psycho or, at any rate, not a dangerous one. Libby was in no doubt that Panom, with his stunt-fighting ambitions, was as barking as Lassie – but he was also totally harmless.

'What on earth is there to laugh about?' Luke asked, rather huffily.

Through her relieved giggles Libby managed to explain. 'He's not a deranged fan,' she finished. 'He's just a sweet old guy looking for his fifteen minutes of fame.'

'Are you sure?' Luke looked doubtful. 'He was shaking when he spoke to me.'

'That's because he doesn't know you! He really thinks you're an action hero. He doesn't know you have manicures and Botox.'

'Hey, take that back!' warned Luke. 'I do not have manicures.'

'Hmm, so you say. And that tan's a bit suspicious, too,' she teased. 'Seriously, though, Panom's OK. In fact, some of the stuff he says is really worth listening to. He can be quite profound. I think I'm going to start taking his advice from now on.'

Luke raised his eyes to heaven. 'You're as bad as Dash with his psychic fixation.'

'I saw that psychic too and she was blooming good,' Libby said defensively. 'She knew everything about me. Just like she did with Dash.'

Luke's lips curled upwards into a mocking smile.

'Oh believe me, she so does not know everything about Dash!'

'She did too,' Libby shot back, fifteen again. 'She knew all about him being in love with someone and she told him to go and share his feelings. So there!'

Luke's grin grew wider. 'Now I really know all that psychic stuff is a crock of shit.'

'It is not! That was really good advice. Nobody should keep their feelings all bottled up; it's totally unhealthy. I said as much to Dash.'

Luke was laughing really hard and clutching his sides. 'Let me get this clear. You've encouraged Dash to follow this charlatan's advice? You seriously told him it was a good idea to declare his love?'

Not liking the way that he was starting to cry with laughter Libby raised her chin. Being with Trin had changed Luke, this much was clear: he'd never been this cynical when she'd known him before.

'Look, why shouldn't Dash tell her how he feels?' she demanded. 'I think it's rather sweet. I don't know why you think it's so bloody hilarious.'

'You would if you knew Dash is gay!'

Libby stared at him. 'What? No, he isn't. He can't be!'

'Oh yes he is, young Libby,' Luke told her. 'It's the worst kept secret in the industry. Dear old Dash makes Graham Norton look butch. Sorry to be the bearer of bad news, Lankster; I know you used to have a bit of a *thang* for him.'

Libby bit her lip hard, determined not to let Luke see how crushed she suddenly felt. Lord, what a wicked waste of teen angst! She really should have fancied Leonardo DiCaprio or Robbie Williams like everyone else at school.

'Well, so what if he's gay?' she said, covering her shock. 'His sexuality doesn't make any difference. He should still declare his love.'

Luke snorted. 'Not to Eastwood Jones, he shouldn't. You do realise that you've just encouraged the poor bastard to tell his director that he's in love with him?'

Her hands flew to her mouth.

'Aha! Now you see the problem. I mean, does

Eastwood Jones really seem like the sort of man who'd take kindly to a same-sex suitor?'

Ten bums in a row! Eastwood Jones was hardly the sensitive type. In fact, he was about as sensitive as a great white shark. He'd go mental and probably punch poor Dash on the nose. And it was all her fault for encouraging him. She was doomed because it seemed that no matter what she did Angela's prophecy kept coming true.

'We've got to stop him!' she gasped. 'Eastwood will flip!'

'What's all this *we* business?' Luke asked. Then, seeing the worried look on her face, he put a hand on her shoulder. 'Don't panic, Libs. Eastwood was going into town this evening so he's miles away from Dash. Nothing will kick off tonight.'

But Libby wasn't leaving things to chance. No way. 'I'm going to make sure he's not camping outside Eastwood's room or something.'

She shot back the bolt and yanked the door handle downwards but the door didn't budge. She rattled the handle frantically but still absolutely no joy. The door wasn't moving.

'It won't open,' said the ever-helpful Luke. 'That must have been what we heard outside. It wasn't your mad friend Panom; it was security locking up for the night.'

Libby slapped her palm against her forehead. Doh! Of course. She'd actually passed the members of the security crew on the path. Now, thinking back, she recalled that the security man had a large bunch of keys on his belt. With a jolt of dismay she realised that she and Luke were locked in for the night.

'Don't look so worried,' Luke said, gently placing his hand on hers and stopping the frantic door-rattling. 'I'm not going to jump your bones. You're way too young for me.'

'Well, you're ancient. At least thirty!'

Steering her away from the door and on to a low seating area, Luke said, 'Thanks for that, Lankster. I'll have you know that lots of women would be delighted to be locked in a caravan with me.'

'Yeah, but I bet none of them have caught you squeezing your spots in their bathroom.'

'Hey, that was a long time ago!'

They grinned at each other. In the darkness it felt oddly intimate and in spite of herself Libby felt a fizz of excitement. Luke was gorgeous and good fun and they were all alone for the foreseeable future . . .

Then he broke the spell.

'Jeez, what is it with Zoe's friends and relatives at the moment? They keep placing me in these compromising positions! Trin will go mental.'

'Why?'

'Because, my innocent lanky friend, this will look terrible if it gets out. If the tabloids got hold of this they'd have a field day. Don't you realise that I live my life in the glare of the media paps?'

Libby digested this thoughtfully. It didn't sound like a whole bunch of fun.

Luke flicked on a lamp and in the buttery light she saw that his eyes were crinkled with amusement at some memory.

'Anyway, going back a bit, what did you mean by Zoe's friends compromising you?' she asked, intrigued. 'Which friends? And what happened?'

'That's my business, nosey! All you need to know is that I ran into Fern in Prague a while back. She turned up at my hotel looking like she'd just swum the Channel. Even her platform boots were filled with water.'

'And? What happened then?'

'It's too long a story to go into now; it'd take hours and hopefully we won't be locked in all night,' said Luke with a wink. 'Besides, it's not a tale for your young ears!'

Libby tried her hardest to get the details out of him but Luke clammed up tighter than an out-of-season oyster.

Her stomach was rumbling – she'd missed dinner after all – so she rummaged around in the fridge but instead of food it was just stocked full of anti-aging creams. With a snort of disgust Libby carted them back to the table. She might as well make the most of a bad situation and give herself a facial. Besides, who knew when she'd see Crème de la Mer again? On her salary she was lucky to afford a tub of Vaseline.

'Please no!' Luke protested, as Libby began to experiment with the tubs of expensive goo. 'This is just like being with Trin. I swear to God she baths in this stuff!'

Libby plunged her hand into the cold gloopy cream. Was it her imagination or was her skin getting smoother already?

'Trin worries about her age,' Luke went on, picking up a tub of eye gel and tossing it from hand to hand. 'It's hard for her being in this business where everyone judges by appearances. She's under huge pressure to look good.'

The pale skin and tight shiny Botoxed face weren't a great image in Libby's opinion, but she kept that to herself. After all, Luke was Trin's partner and probably thought she looked incredible for her age, whatever that *really* was.

'So how did you guys meet?' she asked. They were both in the movie business, but apart from that she couldn't see that they'd have anything in common. Luke, in spite of his fame and success, was easy-going and grounded, whereas Trin was so up herself she was almost inside out.

Luke sighed wearily. 'OK, Libs, here's the rule. What's said in the trailer stays in the trailer. Agreed?'

Instantly her curiosity was piqued. 'Agreed.'

He put the eye cream down and cupped his chin in his strong hands. His startlingly blue eyes, irises ringed with indigo as though an artist had circled them with a fine brush, met hers. Libby was struck by the sadness that swam in the sapphire depths. What on earth did Luke Scottman have to feel down about?

'There are a lot of illusions in Hollywood,' Luke said slowly. 'Dash's sexuality is one good example. The key to success in my world is about building an image, a brand if you like, that people believe in and aspire to. It's all smoke and mirrors really.'

Libby nodded. 'I get that. But you're genuine.'

He pulled a face. 'I try to be, but *Scinity* isn't. I met Trin on a film set when I first started out. We got papped together a few times, which really raised both our profiles and got the film a hellava lot of publicity. Our agents thought it was a really good idea if we kept the momentum going by being seen out and about as a couple. I wasn't really into her because I was still hung up on someone else, but Trin was cool about that. She told me that this was all part of how the film industry worked and that she was happy for us just to be mates.'

Libby was stunned. She'd read *Hello!* and *OK!* and was convinced that Luke and Trin adored one another. They were stock favourites in *Heat* and all the other celebrity mags that Zoe teased her about reading. Everyone knew about their homes and cars and glamorous holidays in the Maldives. They even had an advertising deal for designer watches where they were artfully arranged on a four-poster. And none of this was real? What next? Posh and Becks were *just mates* too?

'Don't look so surprised,' Luke said. 'It happens all the time. Trin was great. I knew nothing back in those days so she took me under her wing and showed me how it all works. In return I just maintained the illusion that I was her partner.'

'But why Trinity Duval?' Libby couldn't help herself. Of all the people to choose for this charade why the self-obsessed and shallow Trinity? Why not someone lovely like Jennifer Aniston? Yes! Jen and Luke would look great together. Take that, Brad!

'Trin's really sweet once you get to know her. Sure, she's a bit image obsessed but she has to be in our business. She's always played it straight with me about what she wants from our partnership, and it's nice to be with someone who understands the pressures of the whole fame thing. It also has the advantage of stopping the press intruding too much into my *real* private life.'

Libby swirled her finger in the face cream

thoughtfully. 'I think I get it. You're just acting another role, aren't you? But what if you meet someone you really want to be with? What happens then?'

He shrugged his broad shoulders. 'I can't see that happening any time soon. There was someone . . . but it's never going to happen. If I can't be with her then I may as well stick with Trin. It's nice for her to have a younger guy on her arm and it would be such a blow to her self-esteem if I walked away from this now, just when her career is starting to really take off.'

Libby was horrified. 'That's a terrible reason to be with someone!'

'But I'm not really *with* her, am I? Besides, I'm fond of Trin in my way. It's lonely being in the film business, always moving from hotel to hotel, set to set, and it's nice having someone in it with you. And,' he raised that trainee Bond eyebrow again, 'we have certain things in common. A shared passion for some things that others find – erm – unsavoury.'

Eugh. *Unsavoury*? Was that some weird sex thing? So they weren't together but they were sleeping together. Colleagues with kinky benefits. 'Anyway, enough of me,' said Luke cheerfully. 'How's your love life? Kissed a boy yet? Or are you still waiting to have your braces taken out?'

'Cheeky!' Libby sank her hand into the pot and scooped out some thick white face cream. Then, before she almost knew what she was doing, she'd flicked it across the trailer at Luke. A huge splodge of hundred-dollar face cream hit him smack on the nose and splattered on to his shirt.

Oh, bollocks! She hoped it wasn't designer.

'Right,' Luke declared, jumping to his feet and snatching a tub of moisturiser from the table. 'This is war!' He wiped the cream from his face. 'You'll be sorry for that!'

Seconds later they were pelting each other with face cream and screaming with laughter. Thick splats flew across the trailer, coating the walls, the seats and Libby and Luke. Finally cowering beneath the table Luke raised his hands in surrender.

'OK, OK, you win.'

Libby stood up and looked at him. 'I let you off lightly, Scottman.'

Then, still laughing and breathless, they surveyed the mess they'd created.

'As the loser, you can clean it up!' Libby said. When he started to protest she raised her half-empty pot and added, 'Or do you want a rematch?'

'God, no!' Luke said vehemently. 'There's only so much grooming a man can handle.' He glanced down at his shirt ruefully. 'This is trashed – Donatella will kill me. I might as well use it to clear up.'

Suddenly, he was pulling the shirt off over his head

and standing before her in all his bare-chested glory. Even though this was just Spotty Scotty, Libby couldn't help gulping. There was no getting away from it: his body was amazing, all smooth skin and gym-defined abs. He'd certainly improved with age.

OMG! If ever there was a reason to take an iPhone pic and whack it on Facebook this was it. Everyone she knew would just die of jealousy! But after what he'd told her about Trinity she couldn't breathe a word to anyone. How annoying.

Oblivious to her admiration, Luke was busy mopping up the mess with his ruined shirt and chatting away about the food fights he'd had in the good old uni days. Apparently Fern had been a mean shot and Zoe was the master at squirting ketchup right across the dining hall. As he spoke of familiar things and people he slid back from being the Luke Scottman of a million heated female fantasies and just became himself again.

Libby yawned and stretched out on the seat. Somehow she couldn't imagine her sensible big sister spattering ketchup about or being silly. Zoe was always so organised and proper. She'd probably come out of the womb demanding her schedule and a BlackBerry.

'You'd be surprised,' said Luke when she voiced this thought. 'Your sister has a wild streak that's a mile wide.'

But Libby didn't believe him, no matter how much he insisted. As Luke reminisced and her eyes grew heavy she decided that Zoe had probably seldom left the library, except to go to lectures. Her last thought before she drifted off to sleep was that there would never be any surprises with her sister. She, Libby, was the wild and impetuous one. Zoe had always been the sensible one. Always.

But if she was going to stop being a danger to men she would have to take a leaf from her sister's book. Maybe even a whole forest.

14

Libby was woken by the sound of jangling keys followed by a click. For a moment she was totally disorientated before she remembered she was locked in the trailer. Peeling open her eyes, she saw she was covered by a cosy cashmere pashmina and that a plump cushion had been slipped under her head. Further investigation revealed slices of sunshine slanting across the trailer on to the sleeping form of Luke Scottman, caressing his cheeks and playing with the matching gold in his hair.

'Luke,' she said sleepily, still feeling groggy. 'Wake up! We've been released.'

Throwing off the pashmina she swung her legs over the side of the bed and sat up, rubbing her eyes and yawning. Catching a glimpse of her reflection in the table-top mirror she was pleased to see that her skin looked amazing, and glowy. That expensive face cream really did work miracles. No wonder all those rich A-listers looked so good; the stuff was like airbrush in a tub. Her cheeks were a little pink from the already intense heat, yesterday's makeup a bit smeary, and her hair all mussed, but it could have been a lot worse. And, besides, the plush trailer was hardly a prison, was it? It was bigger than most of the flats she'd lived in.

'Luke!' Libby hollered. God, she'd forgotten how he could sleep in for England. It had driven Zoe insane when they'd been university housemates. 'Wake up, we've been unlocked!'

Luke sat up and stretched. In the bright daylight his beautiful torso was almost too much and, feeling suddenly awkward, Libby looked away. The confidences and camaraderie of the night had faded with the stars and now they were going to be strictly back to a professional footing. After all, he was a big celeb and she was just a casting agent – one at the bottom of the heap.

Together they made their way from the trailer park back towards the lobby. Luke was still half asleep, but even yawning ungracefully he looked like Brad Pitt's better-looking brother. With mascara-ringed eyes and her messy hair, Libby thought she could be a fantasy figure, too, but an orc or a goblin rather than the heroine of the piece.

She and Luke were just crossing the lobby when the lift doors hissed open and who should come sauntering out but Trin and Craig. Trin looked stunning in a flowing pink maxi-dress and huge floppy white hat and Craig stood just behind her looking ridiculously lush in a tight white vest and joggers.

Catching sight of them, Craig's eyes narrowed and then looked away.

Unbelievable! He really had spent the night with Trin of all people, and after all those lines he'd spun about liking natural women. Trin was as natural as monosodium glutamate! No wonder he couldn't look her in the eye! *If he wants a kick-boxing match today,* fumed Libby, *I'll be first in the queue!*

'Hey, babe,' Luke said easily, dropping a kiss on to Trin's cheek. 'You look good.'

'You don't,' Trin said coldly. Her nose wrinkled, or rather it tried to. 'Eugh. You smell bad. You need a shower. And a shave.'

But as she ran a false-nailed hand down Luke's cheek Trin's attention was less on her official boyfriend and more on Libby, whom she was glowering at as though she'd like to strangle her with some tummy control underwear. *Weird,* thought Libby. Surely if *Scinity* was just a brand thing, she wouldn't care who Luke hung out with? Especially as she was blatantly sleeping with the martial arts trainer. Maybe all the Botox was seeping into her brain. Libby was tempted to ask Trin what her problem was but as Eastwood Jones was striding towards them, shouting into a mobile and waving his arms about like a demented windmill, she bit her tongue. Trin could keep for later.

'Fucking, fucking hell!' the director roared, snapping his mobile shut and whacking it against his forehead. 'That bloody idiot Dash. He's gone and ruined everything!'

Libby went cold to her marrow. Had the prophecy struck again? Had Dash confessed his love to Eastwood and Eastwood buried him somewhere in the hotel grounds?

'What's Dash done?' Luke asked, giving Libby a nudge. 'You guys haven't err . . . fallen out, have you?'

Eastwood looked at Luke as though he was an idiot. 'What? Fallen out? Not yet, but we bloody well will when I see him next. I'd break his neck . . . if he wasn't already injured.'

Trin's hand flew to her glossy mouth. 'Oh, my God! Dash is injured? Whatever happened? Was he mugged?'

'Mugged? I wish. No, for some reason the bloody idiot decided to borrow a scooter and motor down into town last night. In the dark and on those pot-holed roads. What the hell was he thinking?'

'No idea,' said Luke, his eyes big blue circles of innocence and Libby was impressed. This really was good acting.

'I was sitting outside a bar with our producer,'

Eastwood continued, 'and I heard the crash myself. He lost control of the scooter and drove straight into some dustbins. It was carnage!'

Now it was Libby's turn to have her hands fly to her mouth. 'Carnage? Oh, my God. Will he live?' She felt close to tears. Being a danger to men was one thing; causing someone's death was another entirely.

'Oh, he'll survive,' the director said shortly. 'But filming will be held up for a while which will totally screw up the schedule. It's gonna cost a fucking fortune!'

Libby could have slumped to the tiled floor and kissed Eastwood's grubby feet for this news. Dash was alive! She didn't know how bad his injuries were but at least her curse hadn't killed him. Still, Angela hadn't been exaggerating with this danger to men stuff. But how could she avoid men altogether? Apart from joining an enclosed order convent (not really an option for somebody who loved travel and excitement) there didn't really seem to be any choice. If only she could call Angela for some advice. If only she'd brought her own dog-eared tarot cards. She'd never leave home without them again.

While she was frantically searching for a solution, the others were still frantically trying to find solutions to filming the injured Dash.

'Can't we shoot the fight scene sooner than planned?' Craig suggested. 'He was due to have a stunt double, wasn't he? It won't take too long to teach the extras the moves.'

'We can't, son,' said Eastwood heavily. 'The extras have gone.'

'Gone?' Libby echoed. 'What do you mean?'

'I mean they've buggered off!' Eastwood bellowed, rounding on her with such ferocity that she shrank away from him. 'They've gone, vanished, vamoosed! Is that clear enough? I'll never get to shoot my fight scene now. It was the only reason I took this bloody film on in the first place.'

Everyone stared at him in horror. Libby's brain felt like it was on a treadmill. Where on earth could forty extras vanish to? And why would they want to vanish anyway? They'd all been desperate for these parts. Some of them had even come to blows in the waiting area.

Eastwood stabbed a sausagey finger at her. 'And not only have my extras vanished, but so has my casting team. You're the only one I've seen for ages. If you clowns want to keep this contract, *you*, missy, had better bloody well sort this mess out. As far as I'm concerned all this is your responsibility.'

And with this parting shot he stomped away, flipping the phone open again and yelling into it. Libby felt fear pool in her stomach. Oh, Lord. This was bad, really bad.

Sure enough, when she hammered on the doors of the extras' trailers there was no answer. And when she peeked inside, each one was deserted. Horror washed over Libby and she had the hideous sensation that the ground was lurching beneath her feet. How could forty strapping lads just vanish? They were in Thailand, not the Bermuda Triangle. This was nothing short of a disaster. The fight scenes were the largest ones in the production. Too long a delay could lead to the film being cancelled; Libby's company dismissed without pay. Millions of dollars were at stake now as well as the futures of many people. Suddenly it was down to her to sort it out.

'You look troubled, little one,' said a gentle voice at her elbow. 'The weight of the world is a heavy load for only two shoulders.'

Opening her eyes Libby saw Panom Yeerum leaning against the trailer, an expression of concern on his gentle face. Wait until he learned that all the extras had gone. He'd be offering to play all the parts, a bit like Bottom in *A Midsummer Night's Dream*! But what was the point of pretending everything was all right? Maybe the old man would give her some words of wisdom. Heaven only knew she could do with hearing some right now.

'All my extras have done a runner,' she said, her eyes filling with despairing tears. 'They've all gone!'

Panom inclined his wise grey head. 'This I know, little one. They have left for other film.'

'What?' Libby gaped at him. 'What other film?'

'Other film being shot much miles inland. Is called *Bridge Over the River*. Extras go there for many more monies,' explained Panom gently. He tilted his head on one side like a thoughtful grey parrot. 'I show you where if you need guide?'

'Can't you just tell me where they are?'

Panom shook his head. 'Roads are blocked from floods, and planes cannot land nearby.'

Libby groaned. This was all she needed. Panom would probably demand a part in the film as payment for his help. But what choice did she have? Eastwood Jones was on the warpath, and time was money.

'Can we find them?' she asked, hardly daring to get her hopes up.

'This journey has an unknown path. Who knows where it will end?' Panom said sagely.

Wow, that was profound. Could be applied to most things in life. Panom might be mad as a box of frogs but he was a local and knew the landscape well. They might not know if they'd succeed, but she'd be a lot quicker at finding the missing extras with him to guide her.

Agreeing to hire Panom, who looked quietly pleased, Libby then spent a frustrating hour tracking the casting team down: but Tom was ill, Kyle nowhere to be found and Hilary still AWOL, so she had to fix this.

Fan-flipping-tastic, Libby thought despairingly, as she crossed the set for about the fiftieth time. She'd been keen to take on new challenges and prove herself but being single-handedly responsible for the future of the movie hadn't really been part of the plan! For a girl who could hardly remember to put the bins out, this was a step just a bit too far.

But what choice did she have? It was totally her fault that Dash was unable to work for the next few days. In the karmic scheme of things it probably was down to her to sort things out. With a heavy sigh and a refill of Evian she set off to find Eastwood Jones. *Come on, Libby*, she told herself sternly. *Get a grip!* How hard could it be to find a man with a foghorn voice and the physique of the Hulk?

Libby eventually found Eastwood in the hotel gym, breaking every regulation going, by smoking a cigar and drinking Scotch while Craig put several minor cast members through their paces. For a minute she stood and watched as Craig spun and twisted with an impressive mixture of grace and power.

'There you bloody are,' snapped Eastwood when he caught sight of Libby, as though she'd been the elusive one. 'Have you found my extras?'

Libby gulped. 'Not exactly, but I do know where they are.'

'And where exactly is that?'

Nervously she repeated what Panom had told her, the narrative punctuated by the director's bellow of rage that his extras had been poached by a rival production. His outburst interrupted Craig, who stopped his training abruptly and came jogging over to see what was up. Libby felt his gaze on her so tangibly that it was like a caress. In spite of the heat, she shivered. No matter how angry she was with Craig there was something about him that she still found irresistible.

'What's up?' he asked. 'You look bushed, Libby.'

Libby felt bushed. Not that she'd ever admit so to Craig. She opened her mouth to explain the situation but now it seemed she had super ventriloquist powers because the director's voice was speaking instead of her own.

'My fucking extras have been stolen!' Eastwood explained for her. 'They're miles away across the rainforest on some other set and unless we get them back pretty damn quick this whole film will go kerboom! Someone has to go and fetch them back.'

'I'm already on it,' Libby said quickly. 'I'm leaving soon to find them.'

Craig frowned. 'I'm not sure that's a good idea. It's

pretty wild out there and the roads aren't in great nick after all this rain. Besides, you don't even speak Thai.'

'I'll be fine, thanks,' she said coolly, thinking what a shame he hadn't been so concerned about her last night! Two seconds alone with Trin and all thoughts of Libby had been out of the window. Well, she certainly didn't need his concern now, thanks all the same.

'Let me go instead of Libby.' Craig was speaking to the director now and Libby bristled at his firm tone. 'It's not an easy journey upriver and I know this area well. It would make far more sense to send me.'

Of all the bloody nerve. He thought she couldn't handle the challenge and from the look on Eastwood's face he was only seconds away from agreeing. Well, she'd show both of them!

'I've already found a guide,' she told Eastwood, turning her back on Craig. 'He's a local and is going to take me to the other set. We'll leave once it's cooled down a little. So it's all arranged and no one needs to worry.'

Eastwood looked at her approvingly. 'That's what I call initiative!'

'But you can't go alone with a Thai man you don't know. You'll have to take someone with you,' Craig insisted.

'It's not far, only two days' trek,' Libby insisted. The only danger with Panom was that she'd be nagged to death. He'd probably have talked his way into a role in the film by the return journey. In fact, if Panom had his way he'd have been hired to replace Dash *and* the forty extras!

'That's the most ridiculous thing I've ever heard. I'm coming with you. If that's all right with Eastwood,' Craig said firmly.

Eastwood nodded. 'Good idea. If anyone can kick those lads' arses all the way back to my set, it's you.'

Libby was horrified. No way did she want to spend any time in close proximity to Craig. The Trinity thing aside, there was also the prophecy to think of. He'd end up in pieces if the events of the last few days were anything to judge by.

'That's a kind offer, Craig, but—'

'He's going with you and that's an order,' barked Eastwood.

Libby opened her mouth to say this was a film set, not the army, but the steely gleam in the director's eye and the way he'd crossed his arms made her think better of it.

Libby looked from the man in charge to Craig and knew she didn't have any choice. With his hands placed on his lean hips and his jaw set, Craig looked determined to win this discussion and you'd have to be mad to argue with Eastwood. His outbursts made Gordon Ramsay look meek and mild.

'Fine, come then,' she said to Craig. Once Eastwood Jones was out of earshot she added, 'But it's a total waste of your time. I don't need you.'

'Yeah, you've already made that very plain, thanks, dahl,' drawled Craig with studied nonchalance. His eyes hardened. 'Don't worry; I won't be making a pass if that's what worries you. I may not be a movie star but I can take a hint.'

'And what's that supposed to mean?'

But Craig just shrugged. 'Aw, just forget it. I can't be bothered to spell it out. At least we both know where we stand, don't we?'

Did they? She stared at him in confusion. They were so close that she could feel the heat of that strong body and smell the sexy scent of hot male mingled with a lemony aftershave. For a split second she was back on the beach with Craig's arms pulling her close and she almost took a step closer, her fingers itching to wind themselves into his hair. But then she looked up and saw the hostility in his expression and remembered that he was fresh from Trinity's bed. A wave of fury swept through her bloodstream and she clenched her fists to stop herself from physically pushing him away.

'We certainly do,' she said coldly. 'And if I had my way you'd stay here.'

'It's lucky then that our director has more sense than you,' grated Craig. 'You know nothing about

Thailand, nothing about the rainforest and even less about yourself.'

'I know I wish I'd never met you!' Libby snapped.

'Yeah? Likewise! Listen, I can take a knockback so don't worry yourself on that score. I'm not famous; I get it! And I don't get a brass razoo if those extras don't come back. I need my wages so I'm gonna make damn sure we find them. If you don't like it, then tough!'

Libby *didn't* like it. Spinning on her heel, she felt her ponytail bobbing with indignation as she strode away from Craig. How dare he have a go at her? She wasn't the one sleeping with a film star, was she? How dare he assume that she had an issue with that because he *wasn't* a star himself? Had he totally forgotten what he'd said to her before he settled for a richer option? Of all the arrogant, insufferable people she'd ever met he had to take the most insufferable of the lot prize.

As she stomped back to her room to throw some clothes into a rucksack Libby fumed and raged so much it was amazing she didn't explode.

What was it Panom had said again? She wondered as she rode the lift up to her suite. Something about the journey being an unknown path and who knew where it would end? It hadn't filled her with much confidence at the time and now she felt even worse. Because she had a feeling she did know how it was going to end. Badly.

Craig had better watch out. The way she felt right now Libby wasn't so much a danger to *men* as to one man in particular. And if he carried on needling her and making sarcastic comments, she fumed, it wouldn't be long before he found this out.

15

Several hours later Libby stood on a rickety jetty and stared in alarm at the seaplane awaiting her. It wasn't that she had a problem with seaplanes – Libby loved flying and watersports – but this small Cessna had definitely seen better days. Paint peeled from the wings and rust speckled the dented fuselage like freckles on an acne-pitted face. The engine spluttered and wheezed like a forty-a-day smoker.

'Are you sure this thing is safe?' she asked Panom warily. 'It doesn't look like it's flown anywhere since the 1940s.'

Panom, who was already on board, looked most offended.

'Is very, very good plane. Is best seaplane for miles.'

Glancing around at several other rust buckets that were only slightly more dilapidated than the one she was about to risk her life in, Libby didn't exactly feel comforted. Besides, Panom was bound to say this. The pilot was some kind of relative of his, the giveaway being the way he called Panom 'uncle', so obviously he was biased. Watching the plane list to the right as Panom started tending to the moorings she had a sinking feeling that things were only going to get worse from here on in.

'Come on Libby, get moving.' Craig strode past her and lifted their heavy backpacks into the plane as easily as though they were made of feathers. Libby gritted her teeth. Bloody show-off. She could have done that herself; she didn't need him. It would have been worth a shoulder injury just to be able to show the Aussie interloper he really was surplus to requirements.

Pointedly ignoring him, she turned back to Panom. 'I don't see why we can't go by road. Surely it would be safer?'

Panom looked up from his rope coiling. 'Big, big landslide, little one. Much danger. This way quicker. The wings of a bird will fly your troubles far away.'

'Hmm,' grumbled Libby. Panom's deep and meaningfuls were starting to get more and more obscure. 'Why can't we just fly Thai Air? At least they have planes which stand a hope of making it.'

'Lighten up, for God's sake!' Craig said. 'Jeez, I can't believe I had you down as the type of girl who likes adventure. Talk about a whingeing Pom!'

Libby glared at him. 'I do like adventure. But I also

like being alive. Why can't we go in something a little more modern?'

'Because, oh grumpy one, where we're headed to is several mountain ranges away from the nearest airport,' he replied as he climbed into the plane. 'This little beaut can land on the delta. Isn't that right, Panom?'

Panom nodded, still bemused as to what her problem was. 'Is good plane. Safe plane. You come now. Please.'

Uttering a silent prayer, Libby clambered into the tiny Cessna. Craig's hand stretched out to help her but she ignored it.

Inside, the plane was tiny and very basic. Panom was in the cockpit, chattering away in Thai to the pilot, leaving the tiny backseat for her and Craig. Libby tried her hardest not to make any physical contact with him – God forbid he should think she wanted that – but the space was so cramped that keeping a distance was impossible. His strong lean thigh pressed up against hers and his arm was so close that she could practically count the individual golden hairs. As he leaned forward to ask Panom about how long the flight would take, his forearm accidentally brushed against her breast and Libby leapt as though scalded.

'Jeez, you are jumpy,' Craig said.

She ignored him and stared out of the window, desperate that he didn't see that her cheeks were redder than Postman Pat's van.

Then the engine began to rev faster, the little plane shuddering as though mentally psyching itself up for the ordeal ahead. Suddenly they were racing across the glittering blue waves and showering the air with shimmering sea spray. Moments later, the plane gave a lurch like a steeplechaser hurling itself over Becher's Brook and they were up and away.

Libby exhaled slowly as the plane climbed higher and higher into the cloudless sky. At least they were airborne, which was a relief because she'd seriously doubted the ancient plane could really fly, and her hopes started to rise, too. They'd find the extras and persuade them to come back, she just knew it!

But Libby's optimistic thoughts were premature. Just as she was delving in her rucksack for her water, the plane banked sharply to the left and sky and greenery whizzed past the window in a sickening blur. The Evian flew out of her hand and the bag sailed merrily after it, scattering a trail of lipstick, tissues and Tampax across the cabin.

The plane was going down! She knew she should never have got on board such an old rust bucket. What on earth had she been thinking, listening to Panom?

The guy thought he was Jackie Chan, for heaven's sake! It was obvious he had delusions. Why should he be any less deluded about his nephew's plane?

'Chill, Lib. It's fine,' Craig soothed, seeing her white face. 'The pilot was just changing course. There's no need to cut off my circulation.'

Glancing down, Libby realised she was gripping Craig's forearm so tightly that her knuckles glowed through her tanned skin. Oops, that wasn't supposed to happen.

Unpeeling her fingers, Craig cupped her hand in his and said gently, 'Don't look so worried. We're not going to crash; the pilot's just giving us a ride to remember.'

She grimaced as the plane lurched again. 'I'd rather forget this ride, thanks!'

His thumb, warm and dry, traced a path across the back of her hand. For a moment she let it rest there, liking the feeling of having his fingers on her, comforting and reassuring as the plane juddered and dipped. Somehow while Craig held her hand she felt safe. But then a mental picture flashed before her eyes of Craig and Trin exiting the lift earlier on and she yanked her hand away. He had no right to touch her, not after what he'd been up to.

'Do you think they could swap this guy for a female pilot?' Libby asked Craig.

'I didn't have you down for such a sexist, Lib. What you got against men all of a sudden?'

If only he knew!

Thankfully, once the plane was above the thick emerald-green forests the pilot abandoned the aeronautics and the rest of the ride was blissfully uneventful. Thirty minutes later they landed safely on the glassy waters by the mouth of the Chao Praya River and it was all that Libby could do not to kiss the pilot and the plane and Panom too. She was all for extreme sports and stomach swooping lurches of adrenalin but that plane journey was a step too far, even for her.

Turning in his seat, Panom gave them a broad grin. 'Good flight. Yes?'

'Awesome!' Craig grinned, giving him the thumbs up. He looked as bright and breezy as if they'd just flown first class while quaffing champagne. Libby's stomach was still churning and she could have willingly throttled him. Still, there was no way she wanted Craig to know just how scared she'd been so she forced a matching grin on to her own face and echoed, 'Awesome.'

'Now for next part of journey,' Panom informed them cheerfully once the pilot cut the engine. 'We travel to my cousin's village.'

'You mean we're not there yet?' Libby was disappointed. She'd hoped that this was it; they'd hop out of the plane, locate the extras and persuade them to come back and then everything would be sorted.

'So how far away is that?' asked Craig.

Panom shrugged his bony shoulders. 'How far is the road of life, my friend?'

Lost for a response, Craig caught Libby's eye and in spite of her dismay she started to giggle. Getting a straightforward answer out of Panom was impossible. It was like chatting to Yoda.

A small, dilapidated fishing boat was drawing alongside the seaplane with a teenage boy at the wheel who was waving and calling to them.

'This is Lee,' Panom told them proudly. 'He very good boy and will take us upriver to my cousin's village.'

Libby swallowed. This tatty boat made the plane look state of the art. She was starting to regret being so keen to impress Eastwood Jones. Would she never learn?

Panom and the pilot busied themselves hauling the luggage from the cabin before leaping from the plane to the boat. Craig followed suit, as surefooted and agile as the Thai guys, and stood on the deck with his arms held out to Libby.

'C'mon, Lib! What are you waiting for? Let's go!'

His wide smile crinkled the corners of his eyes and in spite of her apprehension about the mode of transport Libby found herself stepping forwards. Then Craig's hands clasped her waist, warm and strong against the bare flesh of her midriff, and he lifted her with ease from the plane. For the briefest moment she was locked against his firm chest and her heart did a little jig.

Nerves, Libby told herself firmly as Craig set her down on deck; that was all it was, nothing more. She was perfectly entitled to feel nervous because who knew what the journey ahead held. The goosebumps that decorated her had nothing to do with the heat and strength of Craig's body or the sparkle of his eyes, and everything to do with tension about the task awaiting her. But, no matter how often she told herself this, her eyes insisted on ignoring any good sense and kept slipping back to Craig as he helped to coil ropes and cast away. Sensing her gaze on him, Craig looked up, eyes glinting with amusement, and winked at her.

Libby turned away quickly, cheeks on fire. He thought she was eyeing him up! How embarrassing was that! Pretending to be absorbed in her iPhone she made a real effort to ignore him, even though every cell in her body was suddenly and annoyingly aware of his presence.

A headache stared to beat against her temples and she closed her eyes, succumbing to the gentle rocking of the boat. It had been such a long day and she was exhausted, that was all. It was heat and stress making her feel so odd and absolutely nothing to do with Craig. The sooner she had her extras back and this trip was over the better. Maybe then life would get back to normal?

16

'Wake up, sleepyhead! We're here!'

For the first seconds of waking up Libby wasn't sure where she was, and sleep dragged her back into muddled dreams. She was so tired from her late night and today's dramas that she'd been happy to drift off with the gentle rocking of the boat.

'Come on, wake up.' A strong hand gripped her shoulder and gave her a little shake. It was no use. Wakefulness returned with a rush. Opening her eyes Libby saw Craig looming above her, his mouth curled into an amused smile. 'Hey there, babe. You were out for the count.'

Libby ground her knuckles into her eyes and yawned. 'I had a late night and I'm knackered, that's why.'

A shadow flickered over his face and his dark brows lifted into an ironic expression, the amusement vanishing like the sun ducking beneath a cloud.

'If you must spend the night with film stars don't

come crying to me about being bushed,' he said sharply. 'It was your choice.'

Libby stared at him. Talk about pots and kettles calling one another black! Of all the bloody cheek to lecture *her* when he'd been with Trinity all night while she'd been trying to protect him from getting his face smashed in by Luke.

Glaring up at him, Libby wished she hadn't bothered.

'Anyway, forget about that,' Craig said dismissively. 'It's time to haul ass. We're at Panom's village.'

Libby scrambled to her feet, suddenly filled with energy after her sleep. Sure enough the boat was moored alongside a spindly jetty adjacent to a ramshackle collection of one-storey huts. Beyond the river's edge she made out the bustle of village life. A group of old Thai men, as worn and wrinkled as old linen, were playing a game of cards while the women tended to chores, small children clinging to their legs or racing round, nimble and bright-eyed, playing catch. *At last!* Libby thought with delight. *The real Thailand!*

Shouldering her bag and following Craig down the gangplank she made her way into the village. Several of the young women looked at her with curiosity. As she passed they inclined sleek black heads and murmured a polite greeting. Libby felt their eyes bore into her back as they stared at her. She supposed that being tall and fair she looked odd to them; this village was so isolated that Westerners were probably a pretty rare sight.

Panom, who had gone ahead of them, was stepping out of the largest hut. A crowd of villagers thronged behind him, hands pressed together, fingertips pointing upwards as they touched their face to their hands and muttered greetings. This was the *wai*, Libby recalled, a traditional Thai greeting and sign of reverence and high regard. Wow, what a warm welcome. She was impressed because everyone obviously had the utmost respect for Panom – but then again these villagers probably hadn't been bugged endlessly for film parts.

'So, so, sorry!' Panom said breathlessly, once he'd introduced Libby and Craig with much bowing and excitement. 'But extras gone! Gone in big, big, hurry!'

Libby felt the blood drain from her face. 'Gone? What do you mean? Where have they gone?'

Craig laid a warning hand on her shoulder. 'What's going on, mate?'

'So, very, very sorry.' Panom looked like he was about to weep. 'This is my cousin's village and film crew were here. Today they move, much upriver.'

'How much upriver?' Libby asked with trepidation.

The pressure was on her to persuade these extras to come back and save the reputation of Cast Away. 'Can we go there now?'

He shook his head sadly. 'The night is soon on us and the river very dangerous. We stay tonight and then tomorrow I show you the way.'

'He's right, Lib,' Craig agreed. 'The river has some really tricky currents. We can't ignore that.'

'But we have to find those extras!' wailed Libby.

Her heart dropped as the enormity of her mission really began to sink in. Should she press ahead with the long trek through the jungle or would it make more sense to turn back now and find new extras? The forty she had found were already trained and finding new replacements and teaching them everything from scratch would take even more time. Time she really didn't have. Even though it took them further away from Hua Hin and the rest of the crew, continuing upriver was the best option.

'The rains are coming,' Panom warned, pointing to a sky that had suddenly bled colour from deepest blue to a murky dishwater. 'You our very special guests! My cousin will show you much honour.'

Libby sighed, resigned to her fate. 'Thank you, Panom. But promise me that we will leave at first light tomorrow, OK? We have to get those extras back as fast as possible.'

'The drum of impatience has a powerful beat,' said Panom.

Libby gritted her teeth. Right now she felt like beating Panom, never mind a drum. She only hoped that he did actually know where the extras were and that this wasn't an elaborate ruse to try and impress her. If she returned without the forty guys they needed, Eastwood Jones would probably bash her brains out with his megaphone. It was not a happy thought.

While she contemplated her sticky end, Craig, who didn't seem in the least concerned about the delay, wandered off to join a group of Thai lads who were having a kickabout. Libby watched him passing the ball to the lads and laughing with them as they wove up and down the makeshift pitch. The lean grace of his fighter's body was almost poetic as he wove through the defence and scored a goal, prompting the Thai lads to cheer and high-five him.

Show-off, Libby thought bitterly. It was all right for Craig. This was just an adventure and a bit of a laugh as far as he was concerned. Eastwood wouldn't blame him if the extras didn't return so no wonder he was chilled out. The director had made it pretty clear this situation was her responsibility and he fully expected her to handle it.

Come on, Libby, she scolded herself. *How hard can*

this be? You're finding some extras, not inventing the wheel. You can do it. Of course you can.

'Come, come!' Taking her arm, Panom led Libby inside the largest hut. This was clearly the social hub of the village and to her surprise Libby saw that a group of guys were watching Chelsea vs Man United on a flat screen, wearing replica kit and drinking cans of lager. Laughing, she accepted a Stella from Panom and settled down to watch the rest of the game.

All she needed was her Xbox 360 and things would be perfect.

The game came to an end as night's cloak spread itself over the village and stars freckled the sky. Panom was holding court and chatting in rapid Thai, the only bits of which she could understand were *Wayne Rooney* and *goal!* Then Man U won and somehow Panom was on the table dancing up and down and cheering.

'We are having a feast in Wayne Rooney's honour!' he explained, seeing her confusion. 'Much dancing. Much celebration.'

Personally, Libby didn't feel much like celebrating but Panom looked so excited she hadn't the heart to say so. Besides, Geminis were party animals, so maybe it was time to indulge in her astrological stereotype?

Glancing out of the door she saw that Craig was still playing football, his sun-streaked blond hair sweeping back from that strong-boned face as he tore up and down. Hmm. She wondered what star sign he was? Fun-loving Aries? Or maybe open-hearted Virgo? For a second she found herself hoping that it wasn't either of these because they weren't supposed to be compatible with Gemini. She gave herself a hard mental slap. What the heck did this matter anyway? She and Craig weren't written in the stars. Apart from the fact that she was staying well clear of men, he had to be one of the most annoying guys she'd ever met.

Feeling disgruntled, she wandered past the football area to a large gathering of villagers who were clustered around three fires. Here the womenfolk of Panom's village were tending a multitude of cooking pots balanced over an open fire. Fragrant steam rose from each bubbling pan and, peeking in, Libby saw that they were making a vast Thai curry. Seeing her looking a bit lost, a couple of the girls took pity on her and beckoned her over. Soon she was in charge of picking out the crabmeat for the main dish. It was an easy enough job and as she worked Libby's thoughts drifted over the events of the past few days. Craig, Tom, Luke and finally Dash had all been touched by the prophecy, she thought sadly, and heaven only knew who the next victim would be. As she picked at the crab her mind picked over the events of the past weeks. Not for the first time she wished that her iPhone worked out here so that she could look up her horoscope.

Libby finished her final crab and was just washing her hands when Craig came striding towards her. His face was flushed from his exertions and his eyes danced with good humour. That was a relief, she thought. He'd been so weird and snappy earlier, almost as though *she* was the one in the wrong!

'Smells good. Never had you pegged as a cook though, Lib!'

It was a family joke that Libby could burn water but she wasn't going to reveal any more failings to Craig. Instead she merely gave him an arch look.

'There's a lot you don't know about me.'

Craig's aquamarine eyes raked over her body. 'You're right there. But I wouldn't mind finding out.'

His eyes shone as her cheeks flushed, and not just from the steam of the curry.

'Did you want something?' she snapped to cover her embarrassment. 'Only I'm busy.'

Craig's gaze drifted to the pile of empty crab shells.

'Yeah, so I see,' he drawled. 'I just thought I'd be a good Samaritan and return your hat.'

'My hat?'

Reaching into his pocket Craig pulled out a baseball cap. Passing it to Libby he added, 'You must have dropped it when we arrived. Surely you recognise it!'

Libby stared down at the cap and her chin practically went splosh into the curry. Craig had handed her a white-and-green baseball cap with Cast Away emblazoned across the top. Of course she recognised it. Tom had got them made up for everyone, Janine had moaned like mad that she wanted pink and Libby had worn hers backwards and made everyone laugh by doing impressions of the Beastie Boys. Hilly had insisted everyone's names were embroidered across the peak so that they didn't get lost.

Yes, of course she recognised the hat. She also knew that she'd given hers to Tom. Slowly she turned the cap over but already she knew exactly whose name would be on it.

'Hilary,' she breathed. 'I don't believe it.'

No wonder the extras had left in such a hurry. Now Libby totally understood why. That hat belonged to Hilary. A moonlighting, bitter and vengeful Hilary, who knew exactly how to hit Libby and Tom where it hurt. Her revenge was so brilliant and so obvious that it took Libby's breath away.

Hilary had stolen their extras!

17

The next morning saw Libby up with the sun. She'd slept well on a small pallet in the hut which belonged to Lee's family and as soon as beams of sunshine crept across the rough floor she was wide awake and ready for action. There was no way she could lay around snoozing. Hilary already had a day's advantage and every second counted.

Although it couldn't be much past six, the air was already pregnant with heat and the vivid blue sky promised yet another burning day. Last night Panom's promised rain had fallen, if indeed rain was the right word for the torrential needle-like torrents which had sliced down into the earth.

This morning, though, it was as if the rain had been nothing but a dream. Peeking through the door Libby saw that the earth outside was steaming and the water of the estuary more glittery than the Swarovski crystal factory. The storm was over which meant that very soon they would be on their way up the river and hot on Hilary's heels. Libby felt a blaze of optimism that was every bit as bright as the scorching sunshine. Maybe her luck was about to change?

Feeling glad she didn't have a sore head after last night's celebrations Libby wandered to the jetty where Craig and Lee were busy making ready for the next stretch of their journey. On seeing her, Craig's face broke into a huge grin.

'Morning, Lib!' he hollered. 'In case you were wondering, I can still walk. My foot isn't broken.'

Libby shot him a look that, in a just world, should have laid six foot of Aussie hunk at her feet. Last night after a glass or three of potent rice wine, she'd tried to join in the dancing only to end up losing her balance and stamping on Craig's foot. Looking at him now, all smiles and good humour *in spite* of the large amounts of rice wine he'd enjoyed, Libby felt like stamping on his head.

'Very funny.'

'Aw, c'mon! You have to admit it was hilarious,' he laughed. 'I had no idea you couldn't dance.'

'I can dance! I just tripped over you. *You're* the one who can't dance!'

'So how come you crippled poor Lee too?' Craig teased. 'I reckon it's lucky for the rest of the men in the village that you gave up at that point.'

'I trod on Lee's foot once,' Libby said. OK, so when

God gave out rhythm he'd missed her. As a child her ballet lessons had been swiftly abandoned.

'He was howling for ten minutes,' Craig said. 'You got his toes a beaut! My ma once told me that men have gotta beware of dangerous girls like you.'

Libby ignored him. Such immature behaviour was below her.

Tuning out his playful comments she followed him down the jetty. At the far end their boat was waiting; the engine was chugging away and belching blue smoke into the bright morning.

'Greetings, little one!' called Panom, hands folded and head inclined politely. 'With a new dawn comes new hope and a thousand opportunities stretch into the horizon.'

'Just what I was thinking,' Craig grinned as he jumped on board. 'A thousand opportunities for getting our feet trampled on, eh, Lib?'

Something told Libby that this joke was going to run and run. She overlooked the teasing and turned her attention to Panom.

'So where are we headed now?' she asked, hopping down on to the deck and pointedly ignoring Craig's outstretched helping hand.

The elderly man gestured upriver where the rain-forest was thicker and already the shrill cries of unseen birds split the stillness.

'I have learned other film is upriver. This film pay much more money. This film need much, much fighters.' He cocked his head thoughtfully. 'Maybe this film like Panom to fight?'

Unless Hilary was casting for *Karate Grandad*, Libby doubted it. Still not wanting to upset Panom, whom she now had no choice but to rely on, she bit her lip and asked instead what he knew of this other film. It was news to her that anything else was being shot in this region and her curiosity was roused.

'Other film far in north,' he told her. 'Big, big film. Much work for my people. Remaking old film about prisoners. I take you there, but is two days from here.'

Libby was horrified. 'Two days? That will set our shooting way back. Isn't there a quicker way?'

'This *is* quicker way,' Panom told her. 'They stay at the Kanchanaburi Hotel. We will find them, little one, I promise.'

And with this Libby had to be content. She really didn't have any other alternative.

The boat chugged up the river with Lee at the helm and Panom guiding. They were heading towards a tributary almost imperceptible to the eye, it was so masked by overhanging vines and reeds.

Looking over his shoulder at Libby, Panom said

proudly, 'Not many know this way. Other English girl never find it.'

Libby smiled at him. 'You're doing a great job. We owe you.'

Panom shrugged. 'The universe is pleased when help is freely given.'

Somehow she doubted that Panom was giving his help for free; he hadn't said much, but she was pretty sure he still had visions of having his name up in lights. He didn't strike her as the type who gave up easily!

Across the deck Craig was busy practising his daily kick-boxing routine. She watched for a few moments as he went through a range of twists and kicks, admiring the fluid grace of the movements and the controlled power of his limbs, before turning away to leave him to his workout.

'Oh!' she gasped, as she almost tripped over Panom who was sitting lotus-style right behind her and staring into space. 'I'm so sorry. I didn't see you there.'

Lee shouted something in Thai and looked so angry that Libby thought she must have trodden on the old man.

'I haven't hurt you, have I?' she asked. Oh, Lord, she must have, because now Lee was jumping up and down and pointing accusingly at her. Now it seemed she was a danger to even old men!

'Very disrespectful! Very bad!' Lee cried angrily. 'Not step on Panom!'

'I'm so sorry!' Libby was mortified. Lee's strong reaction must be because Panom was so important. After all, everyone in the village really looked up to him. He must be a holy man or a guru or something – that would explain all those deep sayings – and she'd just stomped her size sevens all over him. Oh, crap.

But Panom didn't seem angry. Instead he just smiled and said something softly to Lee who scowled but shut up instantly. Then he motioned for Libby to sit down next to him.

'Do not fret, little one. Lee is not angry with you.'

'He isn't?' Libby felt she could be forgiven for doubting this seeing as Lee was still glowering at her.

Panom shook his head. 'Anger like thunder can warn us of storms ahead. In Thai culture stepping over someone is very bad. Very rude. Very disrespectful.'

'I'm so sorry!' Libby was aghast. 'I didn't mean to disrespect you.'

Panom laid one lined old hand over hers. 'This I know.'

Fascinated, she listened as Panom described further the beliefs and customs of his land. There was something really soothing about him – when he wasn't begging for a film role. His soft sing-song voice was really calming and some of his deep comments really did make sense. They sat and talked for ages, while Craig perfected his moves and Libby's skin began to turn rather pink.

Digging her suntan lotion out from the depths of her rucksack she applied it liberally.

'Your culture is so interesting,' she said to Panom when he came to a halt. 'You should write a book.'

Panom looked horrified at the very notion. 'I not write books. I like movies. I big, big movie fan!'

There's a surprise, thought Libby.

Panom was looking at her now with big, pleading, chocolate-drop eyes. 'I like to be in film. Please. I be like Robert Mitchum. I like John Wayne! Get off horse and drink milk, yes?'

She laughed. 'Maybe stick to boats, Panom? I can't see you on a horse!'

While Panom chatted on about his favourite old-time movie stars she sneaked another glimpse at Craig, knowing that she shouldn't. Apart from the fact that he had seriously bad taste in women, he was strictly off limits. If he was injured because of her it really would be the end of not only the film, but also her career as a couldn't help agent. But in spite of her good intentions she couldn't help watching him; his new moves were very strange. It was as though he was slapping himself from head to foot while dancing from side to side. Libby frowned.

'What's the name of that manoeuvre?' she asked, nudging Panom. 'Surely the point of martial arts is that you hit your opponent?'

But Panom didn't get a change to answer because suddenly Craig hurled himself across the deck in true kung fu style, snatched up Libby's suncream and threw the bottle overboard.

'Hey! What did you do that for?' she cried.

'Mozzies!' gasped Craig, slapping his arms furiously. 'Whatever's in that smells really sweet and it's attracted them. They're everywhere!'

He wasn't wrong. Within minutes they were all swatting mosquitoes away and slapping at their limbs. It was only when Panom lit a foul-smelling joss stick and wafted its noxious fumes around that the mosquitoes decided to call it a day. Besides, they were full by then, judging by the amount of bites that covered Libby and Craig.

'Have we got any bite cream?' Craig asked, scratching his arms like crazy. 'These are going to drive me mad.'

Libby shook her head. 'I was in such a rush to leave I totally forgot it.'

'Great, just great,' Craig groaned. 'We're the local diner for the entire mosquito population of Thailand. Hey,' he added to Panom. 'How come you and Lee aren't affected?'

Sure enough the boy and the old man didn't seem to be scratching at all.

'They must have built up an immunity,' guessed Libby.

'Or we taste better.' Craig grinned. But his grin soon began to fade and he began to scratch in earnest. Just seconds later Libby's arms and legs were bubbling with bites and she was practically weeping with the irritation.

Panom took one look at them both before shaking his head despairingly.

'Please, you come,' he said, propelling Libby down some wobbly stairs and into a tiny cabin. She perched on a narrow bunk while Panom rummaged in a box. Craig, who'd followed, stood framed in the tiny doorway with his shoulders totally filling the space. It looked like somebody had crammed an Action Man into a Polly Pocket house.

'Here. You take.' Panom brandished a bottle of vile green goo.

She flinched away, her nose wrinkling in distaste. What on earth was that? It looked like a sneeze in a bottle! 'What's this for?'

'You rub,' Panom explained, miming rubbing lotion over his arms and legs. 'All over body. Bites go away and mosquitos not much like.'

Libby couldn't blame the mosquitoes; she didn't

much like either! When Panom uncorked the bottle the room was filled with such an evil stench that she gagged.

Craig looked alarmed. 'What the hell is in that stuff?'

'Is old recipe. Much secret.'

Libby sniffed. Citronella, eucalyptus and maybe some kind of oil as well? Engine oil, probably, if the smell and viscous texture were anything to judge by. Clinique it was not.

'Do we just dot it on to the bites?' she asked hopefully, but Panom shook his grey head.

'No, little one. You must cover all your body. Lotion will soothe. Soon bites gone.' He thrust the bottle into her hand. 'You must help each other. With four hands is the daily load lightened as the sun lights the world.'

And with this gem of a parting shot he scrambled back up to the deck, muttering about fetching a mosquito net they could share overnight, and leaving Libby and Craig alone in the tiny cabin. Libby was just on the brink of telling Craig not to worry and that she had absolutely no intention of rubbing his body with Panom's green gunk when Craig peeled off his vest and trackies and stood before her in his boxer-shorted glory.

'Jeez, hurry up, Lib!' he was pleading. 'I'm in agony here! I just want to scratch.'

Libby's mouth was dry. He had an amazing body; there was no doubt about it. His perfect skin was the colour of warm honey and dusted with fine golden hair while his well-defined abs knocked Luke Scottman's into cotton socks. How on earth was she supposed to rub lotion all over him and not combust with longing?

Get over yourself, she told herself. *Just do it!* Slopping the lotion into her hands she asked, 'Where shall I put it?'

'Everywhere!' Craig groaned as he scratched his forearm. 'Oh, just do it, Lib, please! I'll be torn to pieces soon.'

So much for keeping her distance. Praying hard to the God of Self Control, Libby began to smooth the green goo all across his back. His skin was warm beneath her fingers, so toned and solid that she almost forgot her own agonising bites. As her hands rubbed the lotion in, Libby couldn't resist tracing the lines of his muscles and her pulse started to race. She was enjoying this. She was trying not to be a danger to men – she'd never claimed to be going for sainthood.

Her face flaming, Libby stopped abruptly. What was the matter with her?

'That's it, your back's done,' she said brightly.

Craig turned around and his eyes glittered with amusement. 'What about the rest of me?'

'The rest I think you can manage yourself,' she told

him firmly. There was no way she was allowing herself anywhere near that spectacular chest. No way at all.

'Spoilsport.' Craig grinned. Taking the bottle, he smothered himself in the lotion until his skin took on a green, rather than a golden, hue.

'That's awesome stuff,' he said, finally finishing. 'Seriously, Lib, it might stink but it's really soothing. I hardly itch at all now. Do you want me to do you?'

The thought of stripping off to her bra and knickers in front of Craig made Libby feel rather faint, but not as faint as imagining how it would feel to have those strong tanned hands running over her body. Oh Lord, she would bet anything that would feel pretty bloody amazing.

She took a deep breath. 'I'll sort myself out. Don't worry.'

He folded his arms across his chest and regarded her through narrowed eyes. 'Want to tell me what your problem is?'

Libby swallowed. 'I don't have a problem. I'd just rather put my own mosquito lotion on.'

Craig stepped towards her. 'I don't believe you. I think you'd love me to lend a hand but there's something stopping you. C'mon Lib, stop being stubborn and do us both a favour. You remember what it was like on that beach just as well as I do.'

And before she could even draw breath to deny it

he'd reached out to cradle her head with one strong hand. With the other he cupped her face and bent to kiss her. Libby twisted her head away so that his lips only grazed the corner of her mouth. But even that slight touch was enough to send a tide of longing coursing through her bloodstream. Corny as it sounded, her knees really did go weak the closer he was.

Either that or the pong from that lotion was making her head spin.

'What's wrong?' Craig said softly. His hand was still on her face, one finger tracing the curve of her cheek. 'Can't you tell me?'

Libby didn't know quite how to explain. It seemed Craig was an addictive new extreme sport, and one that she really shouldn't indulge in. She stepped back, breaking the contact and pushed fronds of hair away from her flushed cheeks. Her mosquito bites forgotten she itched with a different kind of urgency: the need to tell the truth. Tonight, she would have to lie next to him beneath mosquito nets. Unless she spelled it out about the prophecy and the danger he was in there could be huge trouble ahead.

'Look, Craig, there's something you need to know about me,' she said slowly, a small worried frown puckering the skin between her eyes. 'I'm not what you think I am.'

He raised his eyebrows. 'Damn, you're not a ladyboy are you?' he said, mocking her.

She grimaced. 'I'm being serious, Craig. You think I'm this crazy happy-go-lucky person without a care in the world; somebody who does whatever she likes—'

Craig folded his arms. 'How do you know what I think of you?'

'Because that's what everyone thinks of me!' Libby said in despair. 'But there's a hex on me, a real one, and it puts any men I'm close to in real danger. A psychic told me about it and she's absolutely right. I know it sounds crazy,' she added when she saw he was about to speak, 'but there's just so much evidence to back it up!'

Craig stared at her, his brow furrowed, so Libby ploughed on and listed all the evidence for Angela's prophecy, starting with the punch-up at the hotel right through Dash's accident and concluding with the mosquito-attracting suncream.

'So you see,' she concluded eventually, 'there's so much proof that I'm just not prepared to chance it any more. I really am a danger to men. You need to keep away from me, for your own sake!'

But Craig looked far from convinced. 'Seriously, Libby? You can't believe that superstitious rubbish?'

'There's too much proof for it to be a coincidence.'

'But that's exactly what it is! Coincidence. And a bit of bad luck. You jumped too early, that was why our chutes got caught. Your boss drank untreated water so he got sick. And Lee's foot got tramped on because you can't dance. So bloody what? It's nothing to do with you!'

She shrugged. 'Like I said, I'm just not prepared to risk it.'

Craig's eyes hardened. 'So you say. Well, either you're choosing not to use your head or it suits you to see things in a slanted way.'

She stared at him. 'What's that supposed to mean?'

His eyes held her, so strong, and so tainted with hurt that she had to look away.

'What I mean is, if you want to give a bloke the brush off, have the guts to do it honestly rather than making up a pack of lies,' Craig said bitterly. 'You can't come near me because of a prophecy? Yeah, right.'

'It's true!' cried Libby. It was frustrating beyond belief to tell the truth and still be disbelieved. Whoever had said honesty was the best policy ought to be shot.

But Craig just shook his head in bewilderment. 'You're nuts.'

'No, I'm not. Take Panom for instance; he obviously lives by the words of the spirits and he seems happy enough. I want to be more like him. Everything he says is so wise, so profound.'

'Everything?' Craig didn't look convinced.

'OK, maybe not everything. But he's clearly some sort of sort of spiritual leader. Did you see the way the people at his village respected him? I think there's more to him than meets the eye. From now on he's going to be my unofficial guru.'

'Let's get this straight. You seriously think Panom's the next Dalai Lama? Come on, Lib. Get real!'

Craig stared at Libby as though she was crazy. The look on his face said as much and she felt really indignant on Panom's behalf.

'He seems to have a real insight into things.'

Craig snorted. 'Maybe you could ask him to sort out your prophecy problem. Perhaps he could chant it away for you or something?'

Argh! Libby clenched her fists in irritation. She knew violence wasn't the answer, but it would be very satisfying.

'You wouldn't be laughing if you were in my shoes,' she snapped. 'In fact, seeing as you insisted on coming with me to find the extras maybe you shouldn't be laughing either?'

'Because you're such a danger to men? Aw, c'mon Libby. That's a load of old cobblers and you know it.'

Libby glowered at him. Biting back a sharp retort she just said calmly, 'I'm not asking you to believe me. I'm just telling you the way things are. And the way they're going to stay.'

Craig spun around to face her, so abruptly and so fast that Libby took a hasty step back. His acquamarine eyes were dark with annoyance and there was a grim set to his jaw.

'You're incapable of thinking for yourself, that's the problem!'

Lost for words Libby gaped up at him and saw herself reflected in the dark depths of his pupils, a slight figure with wild blond hair and clenched fists.

'You don't want to take any responsibility,' he continued. 'It's easier to blame everything and everybody else, isn't it? That way you don't have to make any decisions. For all you give it about loving taking risks the truth is that actually you're scared stiff. Just admit it.'

'That's bollocks!' Libby protested. 'I'm not scared of anything. Ask anybody! I've done all kinds of stuff. Parachuting with you was one of the easier ones!'

But Craig just sighed and shook his curly head. 'You don't get it, do you? I'm not talking about bungee jumping or sky-diving. I'm talking about the really dangerous stuff – facing up to reality and your feelings!'

And with this parting shot he strode away from Libby, leaving her seething.

18

Who the hell did Craig think he was? How dare he accuse her of not facing up to reality?

'Idiot,' she muttered. And as for saying that she liked to be told what to do? that was nothing short of ridiculous. She'd show him.

Libby turned her back on Craig and consulted her mobile. There was still no signal, which was probably a good thing because it meant that she wouldn't have to receive any irate messages from Eastwood Jones. On the other hand it also meant that she couldn't phone Zoe for a comforting chat, something she could really do with right now.

'Excuse, please.' A small hand plucked at her sleeve and glancing up from her phone Libby saw Lee staring at her with a very worried expression.

'What's up? Is everything OK?'

Lee shook his head. 'The weather. It looks bad.'

Libby glanced over the top of his glossy dark head to the glassy smooth river. Above stretched another cloudless blue sky that glittered diamantine on to the river. If Lee thought this was bad weather then he really ought to live in England for a bit.

'Eh? It's stunning out there,' she said firmly.

'We must stop. Very bad to go on,' Lee insisted, hopping from bare foot to bare foot in agitation. 'Please, Miss Libby. We must stay.'

Sensing Craig watching this exchange, Libby bristled. Now the Aussie guy would think she was waiting for Lee to tell her what to do. Infuriated by this notion, she shook her head.

'We can't afford to lose any time, Lee. I have to catch up with those extras as soon as possible,' she explained. 'Besides, the weather looks fine to me and Panom says we haven't got far to go. Let's push on.'

Lee threw up his hands in resignation and turned to Panom, addressing the older man in rapid and pleading Thai. Libby didn't need to speak the language to know exactly what he was saying – the expression on the young man's face said it all. Panom, however, didn't appear to share Lee's sense of urgency. He merely shrugged before placing a soothing hand on the boy's shoulder and spoke to him in a low and calming tone.

As the small boat continued to chug its way upstream Libby heaved a sigh of relief. She'd proven to Craig that she was more than capable of making her own decisions.

But Libby's relief was shortlived. They hadn't been going for more than an hour when the sky became bruised with swollen purple clouds and the promising sunlight turned a sickly lemon hue. A spiky wind started to blow from the south. Soon the river had turned from a smooth mirror into a mass of choppy waves that tossed the boat from side to side and slapped against the wooden hull. Then the rain began to fall. At first it was just a gentle mizzle, beading Libby's eyelashes and curling the fronds of hair framing her face, but soon it became a downpour so swift and heavy that the sharp drops stung her bare arms. She sent a worried look in Craig's direction, then wished she hadn't. The rain had plastered his golden hair to his head and his white T-shirt clung to him. Libby groaned in despair. Even when on the brink of annihilation he still looked amazing, whereas she probably made drowned rats look stylish.

Clinging to the side of the boat, Libby saw that the river was swelling rapidly, the water rising so fast that their little boat was being swept along at a very alarming rate.

Libby was usually a good sailor; she had raced small Lasers in storm-force winds. But this was something else. The boat was rolling and pitching from side to side now with water occasionally breaching the bow.

Her hands clutched the side of the boat so tightly she could see the knuckles ghostly white through her tanned skin. Oh, God! This was bad. Everything about this spelled disaster, from the strong currents that tossed their vessel about like a toy boat in a child's bathtub, to the grim expression on Lee's face as he tried valiantly to steer to safety. Libby's heartbeat quickened. This was just like *The Perfect Storm* and from what she recalled from that film – apart from the fact that, for an older man, George Clooney looked pretty good in oilskins – it hadn't ended happily.

The boat lurched sharply to the left and oil drums, ropes and nets hurtled towards her. A toolbox gave her a glancing smack on the ankle and Libby cried out in pain.

'Libby! Are you all right?' she heard Craig yell from the far side of the boat. She supposed that now he might actually start to believe that there really was something in the prophecy. This sudden freak and violent storm would be pretty hard evidence to ignore.

The boat lunged to the right and she heard Lee cry out in terror. The rain was filling the deck, threatening to sink the boat.

'We're going to capsize!' she heard Craig shout and saw that he'd abandoned his grasp on the cabin doorframe and was making a beeline towards her. 'Hang on, Lib, I'm—'

But whatever Craig was about to say was lost in a loud crash of thunder, which heralded more of the river swamping the deck. Suddenly water was everywhere and before she knew what was happening, Libby slipped into the fast-flowing rapids. Down and down she sank into an eerily silent and muffled world, the suction of the sinking boat pulling her deep into the grey and murky depths, before instinct kicked in and she began to struggle for the surface.

Arms thrashing and legs kicking, she dodged planks of wood and other debris from the boat, until finally breaking through to the top. Gasping for breath, she trod water for a moment and scanned the churning waves for the others. She was relieved to see that Lee was already at the riverbank. But of Panom and Craig there was no sign.

Oh, dear God. Where were they?

The currents pulled her under and she had to kick really hard to break for the surface again. Coughing and spluttering for air she trod water for a moment before striking out for the shoreline. The current was strong and the swell made her arms scream with pain. Several times her nose and mouth were filled with cold, choking water and she had to stop until she caught her breath, but Libby was a good swimmer and before long she was hauling herself on to the riverbank. For a second or two all she could do was lie there gasping and coughing up brackish water.

Once she could breathe again Libby was on her feet, scanning the river desperately for any sign of Panom and Craig. Eyes blurring with tears, Libby knew that if any harm had come to them because of her she'd never forgive herself.

If only she'd listened to Lee instead of being so desperate to show Craig that he was wrong. If she'd wanted to prove the prophecy was real, then she'd certainly succeeded – but at what terrible cost?

Suddenly she spotted a small dark shape much further downstream. Starting to run in that direction, her bare feet slipping and sliding on the rain-drenched earth, Libby realised with growing dread that this was Panom. Not a strong swimmer like herself he was struggling to keep his head above the water. Rather than being able to reach the bank he was being pulled further and further away by the current.

'Panom!' she screamed, racing downstream towards him. 'Panom, hold on! I'm coming!'

She was just preparing to dive back in when suddenly Craig was powering through the water, his arms slicing through the waves in a strong crawl. Libby's heart rose like a hot-air balloon and she didn't think she'd ever been happier to see anyone in her entire life. Almost unable to breathe, she watched as Craig caught up with Panom, then her hand flew to her mouth in terror when both men vanished beneath the suface.

Please let them be OK. Please let them be OK.

They both came up again seconds later. Craig grabbed Panom and pulled him to the shore. Libby and Lee ran over and took Panom's arm, dragging him on to dry land, and safety.

While Libby kissed Panom on the forehead over and over again and Lee rubbed his old knotted hands warm, Craig stood bent double with his hands on his knees, gasping for breath. His corkscrew curls dripped water into his eyes and his strong arms were pimpled with goosebumps. When he looked up and caught her eye his expression was so bleak that her heart twisted.

'I thought you'd drowned,' was all he said, 'and I couldn't bear it.'

His face was grey and his eyes, usually so merry, were so filled with sadness that Libby fell apart. The next instant, and almost without knowing she'd moved, she was in his arms. Pressed against his body she could hear the heavy pounding of his heart and feel the heat of her skin start to warm his chilled flesh. She was suddenly consumed with the most tremendous relief. He was alive!

'You could have died!' she gasped. There was no strength left in her body and although it was the most clichéd cliché in the book, if he really hadn't been holding her so closely she would have crumpled to the floor like a rag doll.

'I told you I was a danger to men,' she said sadly. 'What on earth am I going to do? I could have killed us all!'

Craig's hands held her face, staring down at her intently as though trying to make sure her features were burned into his memory for ever. 'You've been a danger to me from the first moment I saw you walk out of the darkness and into the firelight. But you knew that already, didn't you?'

Libby did. She'd known it too and tried her hardest to deny it ever since. But now, soaking wet and stranded in the Thai forest, she couldn't hide from her feelings any longer. The prophecy, Trinity, Tom, the missing extras – none of these things mattered for a second as she closed her eyes in delicious anticipation of his kiss.

When it came she felt almost giddy with longing. She felt his warm lips on hers and the muscles of his strong arms tighten as he pulled her close. There by the riverbank, dripping and chilled, Libby's world turned upside down. So used to craving excitement and danger it came almost as a shock to discover that being held safe and cherished in Craig's arms was actually the biggest rush of all.

But then the horrible reality of Angela's prophecy

came racing back faster than the gushing river beside her. She was putting him in danger by allowing them to become closer. She pulled away, looking up into his eyes which were no longer bleak but softened and smiling.

'We can't do this now,' she said softly. 'There's too much at stake.'

His arms tightened around her. 'Suddenly, Lib, getting those extras back doesn't seem to matter like it did. I think a near-death experience kinda has that effect on a bloke.'

Libby reached up and stopped his words by placing her finger over his lips. 'I didn't mean that; I was thinking about the prophecy. I can't risk anything else happening to you. I'd never forgive myself.'

Craig looked down at her, a frown pleating his brow. 'What are you trying to say?'

She swallowed. Oh man, this was just so hard. How was she going to find the strength to step away from Craig when every cell of her being was telling her this was what she wanted more than anything else? Then she recalled the stomach-curdling horror of seeing him vanish beneath the churning water and her resolve hardened. No matter what her heart was telling her, this was a situation where her head had to rule. It might hurt them both right now but in the long run it was far better to be firm.

'I'm saying that this can't happen,' she whispered, her eyes pooling with tears. 'It's too dangerous.'

But Craig just pulled her closer and buried his face in her hair.

'It's too late to worry about that,' he murmured, pressing his lips against her scalp. 'Besides, you've already tried to throw me from a plane and drown me, and both of those things failed. What else could there be?'

Libby wasn't sure, but one thing she knew for certain was that she never wanted to find out what else the prophecy could throw at Craig.

'I know you think it's all coincidence but I can't risk it,' she said. 'I'm so sorry.'

Gently, he pushed her from him, as though just the feel of her in his arms was too much to bear. 'So you just want to walk away?'

She lifted her eyes to his. 'I don't want to. But what choice do I have? How could I live with myself if anything happened to you?'

Craig shook his head. 'I think there's more to this than just some crank's prophecy. I think you're scared.'

'I *am* scared! Bloody hell, Craig! We could have all died just then. What more proof do you need?' Libby bit her lip and stepped back. There was no way she could weaken now. If he took her in his arms and kissed her again she'd be lost, and he'd be a goner before you could say *crystal ball*. 'I'm sorry but until this is over we're better off apart.'

He sighed and, reaching out, took her hands in his, smoothing her cold fingers and kissing them. As his lips danced across her skin Libby shivered with longing so acute that she had to snatch her hands back.

'Please, don't!' she pleaded.

Craig sighed. 'Lib, I can't pretend to understand any of this. And I certainly don't believe in it, but if you want me to back off then I will. I've never had to force anyone to be with me and I'm not about to start now.' He glanced across to where Lee was trying to make a fire out of twigs. The rain was easing off at last so he stood some chance of success. 'Have things your way. I'm going to see if we can get a fire going. Panom looks cold.'

Silently she watched as he walked away from her, his lean narrow-hipped frame taut with suppressed emotion, then she exhaled slowly. Why were things so flipping complicated? Who on earth had she offended in a past life? Feeling really depressed she tore her gaze away from him and went to sit with Panom.

'Walk away from the readied weapon. Things that fire, may also backfire,' said Panom slowly. 'The bright furnace will burn as well as warm.'

Well, that tells me then, thought Libby sadly. This

time his cryptic words couldn't have been plainer. The old Thai man was beyond wise and she'd have to be really old – almost ready to consider Botox – to come close to his level of understanding. This time she would really have to listen to him and bide by his advice. She'd have to be bloody stupid not to.

She glanced across at Craig, coaxing a fire into life with an intent look on his chiselled face, and a lump the size of a rugby ball leapt into her throat. Sensing her gaze upon him he looked up and smiled questioningly. Libby gulped and looked away.

Forget rock climbing and paragliding: staying away from Craig was proving to be the hardest and bravest thing she'd *ever* had to do.

Libby was exhausted. The storm and the loss of the boat had been the realisation of her worst fears. It was only down to luck and Craig's swimming prowess that no lives had been lost. If she'd listened to Lee's warning about the weather instead of being determined to prove herself, then they might have been behind schedule, but they wouldn't have been paddling up this fast-flowing river on a makeshift raft.

Last night they had slept around the fire and had just about managed to keep warm. Sleep had been easy to find, even on the bed of damp leaves she'd made, as the adrenalin flow had stopped and left her done in.

They'd been rowing for the better part of the day and her arms were trembling with the strain of trying to guide the simple craft, fashioned by Craig and Lee from boat debris and driftwood. Although last night the storm had ended as abruptly as it has begun and today the sun now beat down from a cloudless azure sky, the river was still swollen from the heavy rain. By the time they finally rounded a bend in the river and saw the Kanchanaburi Hotel almost every muscle in her body was screaming.

The high white walls of the hotel shimmered in the afternoon heat and through the latticework she glimpsed fountains playing in the sunshine and courtyards filled with shady trees. The humid heat hung heavy and oppressive and she longed for nothing more than to dive into the cool waters of the hotel pool to escape the ruthless sunshine. Only her grim determination not to let Hilary beat her kept Libby paddling. When they finally drew up against the hotel jetty and Craig helped her on to dry land she could have wept with relief.

Libby was so weary from their hard journey upriver that for once she didn't protest when Craig offered to help her ashore. With one arm around her waist, he guided her through the gateway and into the lush hotel grounds.

In spite of her exhaustion Libby still gasped at the beauty and opulence of the exotic surroundings. The path that coiled its way through the bright wisteria flowers and cypress bushes was made of solid pink marble threaded with deep veins of rose and amber while the collection of low-rise chalets sprinkled throughout were more like small palaces than hotel rooms.

And this was where the cast and crew of *Bridge Over the River* were staying? Wow! She was clearly working for the wrong film company.

Still shaking with fatigue, they made their way into the hotel lobby. This grand reception area was staggeringly lavish. A huge crystal chandelier twinkled down from a vast vaulted roof and the walls were richly painted with frescoes of Thai landscapes. But it wasn't this that made Libby gasp, but rather the extreme sensation of déjà vu: standing right before her in the lobby area of the second-most plush Thai hotel were Tom, Trin and Eastwood Jones! The sun must have been so intense she was hallucinating, Libby thought, rubbing her eyes; the sooner she had a lie down the better!

But no, her eyes weren't deceiving her. Sure enough all three *really were* in the lobby. What on earth was going on?

'Sweetheart, I've been frantic with worry!' Tom strode forward and pulled Libby into his arms, pressing a kiss on to the top of her head. Gone was the vomiting wreck she'd last seen, and in his place the uber-cool casting agent, suave and groomed in a white linen suit and acid-green shirt. Releasing her, he took her hands and stared down at her with a frown. 'Where the hell have you been? My goodness, you look an absolute fright.'

Libby wasn't surprised to hear this because an absolute fright was *exactly* what she felt like. Well aware that Tom was laying his concern on with a trowel for Craig's benefit she wriggled out of his arms and demanded to know how they had got here.

'The roads cleared and we were able to get a flight out,' Tom explained. 'There was no way we could wait any longer for the extras and nobody had heard from you, so we decided to set off.'

'I've been in the middle of the rainforest! I don't know whether it's escaped your notice but mobile phone masts aren't exactly in abundance.'

He shrugged. 'Yeah, I guess so. But like Eastwood says: time is fucking money. We need to take ourselves over to that set right now.'

Sunburned, tired and still traumatised from the boat's sinking, it took every inch of Libby's self-control not to punch Tom on his perfect nose. How dare he stand there looking like he'd just strolled out of an Armani advert when she'd spent days struggling to get this far? And now he was demanding that she carried on the search without even so much as a drink of water! The man was so totally selfish that the words *Tom loves Tom* probably ran right through him like seaside rock!

'Calm down, mate! Can't you see Libby's all in? I'm sure you're stoked to have got this close to the extras, but she needs some rest.' Craig stepped forward and placed a protective hand on her shoulder. Libby leaned against him gratefully. Her legs felt like soggy string and suddenly she was really desperate to sit down. It was good to have Craig on side. He understood exactly how she was feeling, whereas Tom didn't have a clue. In fact, she realised with a jolt, he'd never had a clue. He hadn't even been interested enough to look for one.

Tom's eyes narrowed as his gaze rested on Craig's hand. Sensing the animosity between the two guys Libby gently moved away from his touch. The last thing she needed right now was Tom getting jealous and irate again. She was also only too aware that she'd encouraged Craig earlier by kissing him and could sense him bristling at Tom's proprietary behaviour.

'I wouldn't dream of asking Libby to continue without a rest,' Tom said icily. Then, pointedly turning his back on Craig, he added to Libby, 'There's not much room left at this hotel but luckily Trin, Eastwood and I have managed to book the last three suites. You can share with me.'

Libby stared at him. For somebody with an Oxbridge education Tom really was incredibly thick sometimes. 'I'll find alternative accommodation, thanks.'

He reached out and tried to take her hand, missing

when she dug her fingers deep into the pockets of her combats. 'Come on, Libby, don't be like this. You've made your point.'

Libby's blood began to boil until it was about the same temperature as the molten blue sky. 'And what point is that?' she demanded. 'The point that after everything that's happened I don't want to be with you any more? Please, Tom, just get the message. It's over!'

Turning on her heel, she stalked away from him, out from the chill of the air-conditioned lobby and into the warmth of the gardens. Heading towards the shade of a plane tree she took a few deep breaths and tried to calm her rising temper. She wasn't really bothered about Tom. It was his arrogant assumption that she'd just been in a girly strop and would soon come trotting back that was infuriating. What had she ever been thinking, wasting her time on such a tosser? Hilly was welcome to him! In fact, not even Hilly deserved a slimeball like Tom, and that was saying something.

'Lib, wait up!' Craig sprinted down the marble steps from the lobby and with just a couple of strides had caught her up. 'Jeez, woman! Can't you stay still for five seconds?'

Libby grimaced. 'I had to get away. I was seriously about to become a danger to Tom!'

His aquamarine eyes twinkled. 'History, huh? I'm guessing that's your ex?'

She nodded. 'I'm not sure he's got the message, though, and tempting as the thought of a soft bed and a cool shower are, if being with Tom's the cost I have to pay, then the price is far too high.'

Craig reached out and circled her slender waist with his hands, drawing her closer against his chest, so that she had to tilt her head to look up at him. His eyes, thickly fringed by dark lashes, stared down at her and something in their depths made Libby's pulse race.

'Why don't you stay with me tonight?' he asked, his voice husky with emotion. 'We could camp on the beach under the stars, just you and me.'

'Just camp?' she whispered, her heart skipping a beat as his arms tightened their grasp.

'And talk,' he said softly. 'If that's what you want. I'll never ask any more of you than you want to give me. That's a promise.'

He was holding her so close. As she gazed up at him Libby knew with a sudden and terrifying clarity that she wanted to do so much more than just talk to Craig. She wanted to kiss him, passionately, for hours.

Libby didn't think she'd ever wanted anything so much in her life. For a split second she was sorely tempted, but then Angela's words echoed through her memory and she felt again the agonising horror of seeing Craig's head vanish beneath the swollen river water. She couldn't be so selfish as to endanger him.

Putting both hands against his firm muscular chest Libby pushed him away gently.

'I can't,' she whispered. 'I'm so sorry.'

His arms released her instantly. 'Don't do this, Libby,' he warned. 'Don't keep on running away.'

'I'm not running away! Can't you see I'm trying to protect you,' she cried in frustration but Craig wasn't having it. His mouth hardened into a mocking smile and he shook his head slowly.

'That's rubbish and you know it.'

'It's the truth! And besides, I can't go getting involved with anyone. I've still got issues with my ex – you saw that for yourself.'

Craig's eyes narrowed. 'Stop making excuses. Just admit it. You're terrified about how you feel. You weren't bothered about curses and exes a few minutes ago and you weren't bothered when you spent the night with Luke Scottman either!'

Libby stared at him in shock. 'I've never spent the night with Luke. He's just a friend.'

'Aw, come on, Lib! I'm not an idiot! I saw you two arrive in the lobby that morning. You were still wearing the same clothes.'

That was true. But they hadn't been making love, just making a mess.

'You're not even going to deny it,' said Craig wearily.

For a second she toyed with the idea of explaining exactly what had really happened with Luke but then she thought maybe it was better this way. If Craig thought she was shallow and so easily impressed by film stars she was happy to sleep with them on a whim, then perhaps he'd back off? It might hurt her horribly but at least that way he would be safe.

'Think what you like.'

'And what about us?' Craig was staring at her, his face taut with hurt. 'Did none of it mean anything to you?'

She took a deep breath. If only she had a smidgen of Luke's acting talent.

'It shouldn't have happened,' she said. It wasn't a lie, but it was killing her to say it.

This answer seemed to infuriate Craig.

'D'you know what I think, Libby? I think that's just another of your excuses,' he said, so softly that she almost had to strain her ears to hear him. Although he didn't shout, his anger was palpable. 'You're using all this crap about prophecies and exes to protect yourself because deep down you're scared of getting involved with anyone. And I'm pretty bloody tired of the whole thing! I tell you what, Libby, let's just forget it, shall we? Then we'll both know where we stand.'

His sudden rage shook Libby more than she liked to admit. Dismayed, she watched Craig storm off towards the hotel bar and to her horror her eyes swam with tears.

Craig had said she was scared. And he was right. She was scared; but quite what of, Libby wasn't sure. As she watched Craig walk away with every line of his beautiful body screaming fury, her heart plummeted faster than a base jumper with no parachute.

Libby couldn't compete with Angela in the psychic stakes but she had a very, very bad feeling that her violent attraction to Craig wasn't destined to end happily.

20

For a few seconds Libby stood rooted to the spot. Part of her wanted nothing more than to tear after him shouting that she was going to ignore the prophecy from now on. Luckily the stronger part reminded Libby there was far too much evidence to suggest that if she and Craig grew closer, the only thing that would follow would be tragedy. If she really had feelings for him, and from this hideous churning deep inside she suspected this might be the case, then the best thing she could do was stay right away from Craig no matter how much that was going to hurt.

With a heavy sigh, she headed back to the hotel's lobby. This time she was oblivious to the gorgeous flowers and heavy scents because all she could feel was a grinding heaviness in her heart.

'This journey has an unknown path. Who knows where it will end?' asked Panom from his cross-legged position beneath a jacaranda tree.

Libby was about to tell him that the only way her

journey was destined to end was in certain disaster, when a chocolate-gateaux-rich voice replied, 'The end is never known where there is no end.'

Turning around, Libby saw that none other than Luke Scottman was striding over and waving at them. Of course! Luke was shooting a cameo in *Bridge Over the River*. That was why he was in Thailand and had been able to scoot over to visit Trin. Here he was looking bronzed and beautiful in his crisp white shirt and faded blue Levis as though he'd just strolled out of a romantic novel. Libby was suddenly really conscious of her matted hair, sunburned forearms and scruffy combats. Lord, she probably really smelled too after her dunking in the river. Hanging out with perfect A-listers didn't do a lot for a girl's self-esteem, that was for sure.

'What *are* you two talking about?' she asked him, intrigued. Whatever it was it had certainly had a great effect on Panom because the old man was beaming like a Halloween lantern.

'Ah. But much can be divined from the present location,' he told Luke wisely. Or at least, like everything else Panom said, it sounded wise. Libby hadn't actually got a clue what he was on about.

Luke though was nodding and smiling. 'It's hard to divine anything when you've had your ass kicked,' he told Panom.

Eh? Libby knew she was tired but this was becoming seriously weird. The pair of them sounded like they were reading from a script rather than having a proper conversation. As she puzzled over the meaning of Panom's words the two men were laughing and bowing to one another while continuing to banter strange and disjointed sentences. Looking from Luke to Panom, Libby thought it was almost impossible to tell which man was looking more delighted.

'What on earth are you two saying?' she demanded when they finally paused for breath. 'Luke, since when have you been able to quote religious texts? Have you become a Buddhist?'

Luke looked puzzled. 'What makes you say that?'

'All these mantras you and Panom know; is it some Hollywood thing that you've taken up, like Kabbalah, or wheatgrass or Botox?'

He roared with laughter. 'Libby, you are priceless! Apart from the fact that I honestly don't do Botox, no, I'm not a Buddhist. You haven't seen any of my films, have you?'

Oops. Guilty as charged. Much as Libby loved action movies she'd never actually got round to seeing any of Luke's. Every time she and Zoe went to the movies, her sister preferred to watch a rom com rather than one of Luke Scottman's kick-butt flicks.

'If you had,' Luke continued, wagging a stern finger at her, 'you'd recognise the lines from *Buddhist Assassin*! I'll have you know that the franchise is quickly becoming a cult classic.'

Libby stared at him. Suddenly the world was dipping and rolling around her alarmingly. *Buddhist Assassin* and the two films that followed had shot Luke to stardom. He'd even co-starred with Trinity in the latest one, which had sent their fans wild. People loved those movies. And what did Panom Yeerum love more than anything?

Movies, of course!

'We're quoting lines from the film, silly!' Luke grinned, ruffling her hair. 'Panom here's one of my biggest fans. Can you believe he practically knows every word? It's amazing!'

But Libby felt far from amazed. *Horrified* would have been a better adjective. There she'd been thinking that Panom was Thailand's version of the Guru Nanak, hanging on his every word and thinking he was so wise, and the reality was he was a geeky super-fan. Every word he'd spoken, which she'd believed was so cryptic and deep, was just a line from a movie!

She closed her eyes and groaned. How could she have been so gullible? Why hadn't she trusted her first instincts which had told her he was bonkers? The answer to this was that she'd been delighted to think she'd found some kind of guide who could advise her, just as she'd been only too quick to pin all the events that had unfolded recently on to Angela's prophecy. What if the whole prophecy business was as insubstantial as her belief in Panom? What if she'd rejected Craig because of something that wasn't true? Craig had accused her of wanting to be told what to do and he'd been right. Why hadn't she been able to spot this sooner?

'Hey, don't look so worried. I'm only teasing,' Luke said, seeing and misinterpreting the horrified expression on her face. 'I'll get my agent to send you a box set of the *Assassin* trilogy, if you like.'

'Great,' said Libby weakly.

'Not that you need to watch them with Panom here!' Luke said, clapping the beaming Thai man on the back. 'He knows every frame off by heart.'

'So very honoured to talk to you, Mr Scottman,' Panom said. He actually looked close to tears as he said this. Libby felt quite close to tears herself. 'Is big, big dream of mine to be friend of Luke Scottman.'

'See? Some people actually appreciate Spotty Scotty.' Luke grinned. 'Look, why don't you two superfans get freshened up and join me and Trin later for dinner?' Pulling a mock serious face he added, 'We can talk more about how great I am!'

'It'll be a short conversation then,' Libby said drily.

'Anyway, it's a nice idea, Luke, but we won't be staying. This hotel's full apparently.'

'Then stay in my suite. Honestly, it's vast. Way too big for just me and Trin. The sofas in it are plenty big enough to sleep on and we've even got his and hers showers and plunge pools.'

'Thank you! Thank you!' Panom was practically kissing Luke's feet. 'So kind. And we so very tired.'

Glancing at him Libby could see that Panom's lined face was grey with exhaustion. It had been a long and gruelling few days, and if her own fit young body was aching and crying out for rest then she dreaded to think how the elderly man must be feeling. Outside, night's indigo shawl was beginning to wrap itself across the sky. It was late; everyone was exhausted and at least she knew exactly where the extras were now. She could hunt them down tomorrow. Accepting gratefully, she followed her film star friend to his luxury suite. To everyone else it must look as though she was being swept off her feet by one of the world's most desirable men. Catching envious glances from female guests and cast members Libby couldn't help smiling at the irony. Luke Scottman, the man who inspired a thousand female fantasies, had offered to let her sleep in his bed and all she wanted to do was sleep! *Heat* magazine would never believe it!

*

Luke and Trinity's suite was the last word in luxury. While Panom headed off to find Lee and set him up in the suite with them, Libby busied herself exploring. *Help yourself to everything!* had been Luke's parting comment and Libby, feeling grungy and in need of some pampering, was only too happy to take him up on the offer. After a deliciously long shower, so powerful that the jets had tingled like a delicious massage, she'd smothered her body in Jo Malone basil, lime and mandarin moisturiser and played around with a variety of face packs and anti-aging products. If Trin used all this lot on a daily basis it was a miracle she didn't look like a teenager! Libby smoothed some on to her face and then went to explore the mini-bar.

Minutes later she was curled up on the vast four-poster bed, filmy muslin drapes billowing in the breeze stirred up by the air conditioning, and asking the receptionist to put her through to London. More precisely, her sister Zoe.

'Hey, Zoe,' Libby said nonchalantly. 'You'll never guess where I am?'

Her sister laughed. 'I gave up guessing what you were up to a long time ago. Now let me think. Hanging off a cliff? High up in a tree? About to base jump from Niagara Falls?'

'Nope.' Libby paused for dramatic emphasis. 'I'm in Luke Scottman's hotel room!'

There was a silence.

'Luke Scottman, the film star. Blond? Gorgeous? Your old friend from uni?' Libby pressed when her sister failed to reply. 'My God, you should see him now, Zo! Luke's way hot these days. You do remember Luke, don't you?'

'Of course I do,' Zoe said quietly.

'Well, he's here! In Thailand and we hooked up. Isn't that a blast?' When her sister failed to respond she added, 'You might sound a bit more interested. I'm staying in a movie star's luxury suite. It's amazing!'

'Good, well, have fun,' was all her sister said and Libby frowned. She knew there was a time difference but did Zoe really need to sound so disinterested?

'Luke's let me borrow the suite, which was really kind of him,' Libby told her. 'The hotel's fully booked but he said there's enough space for loads of us in here. His girlfriend probably won't be too impressed to see me, an old fellow and a young Thai lad here for the night though!'

'Oh!' Zoe sounded relieved. 'He's lent you a bed for the night! That sounds just like Luke. For a minute there I thought . . .' her voice trailed off.

'You thought I was shagging Luke? Gross, he's way too old,' giggled Libby.

'Thirty isn't old, you know!' Zoe protested, laughing

now. Then she added, casually, 'What's Trinity like? Are they happy together?'

Libby was just about to swear her sister to secrecy and explain how things really stood between Luke and Trinity when the suite door flew open and there stood the actress herself, a look of abject horror written across her perfect features. Hastily promising Zoe she'd call back, Libby hung up and smiled at Trinity.

'Hi,' she said warmly. 'I hope you don't mind me being here. Everywhere's booked solid and there was nowhere else free.'

Trin didn't reply. Instead, she just remained framed in the doorway. Without her parasol-holding Thai attendant beside her she looked oddly diminished. She was dressed from head to toe in the most gorgeous designer fashions, yet somehow she seemed crumpled and dejected. The arrogance and fire that had been a trademark were missing, and Libby thought that Trinity looked sad and rather lonely.

'It's you again,' Trinity said slowly. Her bright eyes swept over Libby and clearly noticed that she was just wearing a bath robe and had piled her wet golden hair on top of her head with a jewelled clip.

Oops, Libby thought as her face flushed guilty. When Luke said to help herself to whatever she needed he probably hadn't run it by Trin first.

'Luke let me freshen up here,' Libby started to

explain, but Trin didn't want to hear it. Holding up a hand to stop Libby's flow of words the actress then began to pace the room, her fists bunched and her bright white teeth worrying her bottom lip.

Libby watched her. The pacing and worried expression were strange reactions coming from a woman whose relationship was just for show. If she didn't know for a fact that Luke and Trinity's relationship was a sham she'd think she was jealous. Trinity's eyes were suspiciously bright too and it wasn't as though there were any cameras hidden in the room requiring the whole broken-hearted girlfriend act.

Unless. . . .

Unless it *wasn't* an act on Trinity's part! Oh, God. In which case, Trinity would now have the worst suspicions about her and Luke and be suffering the unbearable pangs of a broken heart.

Unable to stand this thought, Libby leapt from the bed and tore towards the pacing actress, protesting over and over again that no matter how it looked there really wasn't anything going on between her and Luke.

'I swear to God that Luke is just a friend.'

Trinity regarded her through narrowed eyes of arctic blue. 'So you say, but you seem to be spending an awful lot of time with Luke for somebody who isn't interested in him.'

'I've know him for years. He went to uni with my

sister.' It was clear that Trinity wasn't convinced. 'For God's sake! I don't give a stuff about Luke flipping Scottman, it's Craig I'm interested in!' blurted Libby in frustration.

'Craig?' The perfect features were blank and Libby felt close to screaming.

'Tall and blond? Aussie? Does martial arts? You went to bed with him a few days ago? Ring any bells?'

Trin's facial expressions contorted from incredulity to scepticism to quizzical to surprise to astonishment. Libby was quite taken aback. She hadn't realised Trin had such range. Really, she had been under-utilised as a comedy actress!

With a toss of her blonde extensions and a derisive snort Trin said, 'I haven't been to bed with Craig, you stupid girl.'

Libby stared at her. Was it her imagination or was the teak floor of the suite suddenly starting to pitch and roll like their capsizing boat from the previous day?

'But I saw you!' she whispered. 'You went up in the lift with him one evening and then I saw you together in the lobby the next morning.'

'I've been taking martial arts lessons,' Trin said wearily. 'I don't stay a size zero through willpower alone you know. Craig's been teaching me all the moves I need to keep toned. It certainly beats Pilates.'

'So nothing happened? Are you sure?' Libby

couldn't quite believe it. How could any woman be alone with Craig and not find herself having daydreams about that gorgeous fit body?

But Trin just rolled her eyes. 'Of course I'm sure. Oh, he's attractive, I'll grant you that, but he's a bit too young, even for me! And even when I did flirt with him, he didn't respond. Far too professional, I suppose.'

The straw Libby was about to clutch drifted out of reach. 'So why flirt with Craig if you weren't interested? What's the point of that?'

The actress shrugged her slender shoulders. 'It sounds stupid, but I guess I just wanted to see if a man would actually be interested in me. Although you're probably wondering why I'd want to even play a silly game like that when I'm dating Luke, aren't you?'

Libby said nothing, not wanting to break Luke's confidence, and Trin looked at her thoughtfully.

'Luke's told you the truth about us, hasn't he?' she said slowly.

Libby nodded. 'He explained that you guys just have a business arrangement. He said you're like a big sister to him.'

On hearing this Trin wailed and covered her face with her hands. 'That's exactly how he sees me! I'm some asexual creature rather than a love interest.' As though unable to bear this thought, she strode to the bar and poured herself a large vodka, which she then knocked back in one gulp. Libby was impressed. She hadn't necked a drink like that since college.

'Every man I meet is starting to look at me like that,' Trin continued sadly, her eyes wide and mournful. 'It must be because I'm getting on. Pretty soon the only parts I'll be cast for will be The Kooky Mom or The Older Friend. And then my career will be over. No man will ever want to date me again!'

'That's bollocks! You look fantastic,' Libby said. Well, Trin did look good for someone who was pushing forty and had seen more Botox than Jordan's forehead.

But Trinity was beyond listening to any soothing words Libby might offer. She was far too busy peering at her face in the mirror and stretching her skin taut with her forefingers.

'You should have seen the way your Craig looked at me when I ran my hand along his bicep. I may as well have been his mother! It's over for me. My looks will go, then my career and then everything else. I might as well be dead!' This soliloquy delivered, Trin flung herself on the bed where she pummelled the pillows with her fists and sobbed noisily.

Libby wasn't quite sure what to say or do. On the one hand she was over the moon to hear that nothing had happened between Trinity and Craig, but on the other she was horrified to see the actress in total meltdown. Hesitantly, she perched on the edge of the bed and put a hand on Trin's shaking shoulder, patting and soothing her until after a while the sobs began to quieten. Then she padded to the bathroom and fetched some tissues so that Trin could blow her nose and wipe her eyes. The beautiful lacy white pillows were stained with foundation and mascara and poor Trin herself looked like she'd been trying to copy Alice Cooper. Gone was the haughty Hollywood star, and in her place a sad and broken-hearted woman.

'God, I'm so sorry,' Trin choked, blowing her nose and mopping her eyes. 'What must you think of me?'

'I think you must love Luke very, very much,' Libby said softly.

Trin fixed her with tear-filled eyes. 'Oh God, I do. I've loved him since the first moment I saw him. It was my idea that our agents hooked us up. I thought that might give us a chance of getting to know one another. But it's never been any more than just another acting job for Luke. He doesn't see me in *that* way and I'm starting to think he never will. What will I do then? It's breaking my heart because none of it's an act for me.'

'Why don't you tell him the truth?' It seemed obvious to her, but Trin gave her a watery smile at this thought.

'You're so young,' she sighed. 'Luke would run a

mile if he really thought an old hag like me was in love with him. I mean, look at him. He's gorgeous. He could have anybody.'

The actress was far from an old hag. Most guys would jump at the chance to be with somebody as stunning as her. Luke might be great fun but he was still a guy and therefore programmed to think like the rest of them. Besides, when he'd talked about Trin in the past he'd seemed genuinely fond of her. Surely there was hope?

'I'm afraid not,' Trin sniffed when Libby voiced these thoughts. 'He's had quite a few subtle flings. I'm pretty sure he was seeing someone when he was shooting in Prague although he'd never say. I panicked when I saw you just now because I've never seen him with the same woman twice. That would be something totally different and *Scinity* would be well and truly over and then I'd have lost him forever.'

'But it's such a waste,' Libby cried, genuinely moved by the other woman's distress.

Trin raised her tear-stained face. 'Of course it is, but isn't life full of wasted chances and things unsaid?'

For a moment Libby closed her eyes and saw Craig again, his eyes soft with tenderness as he pleaded with her to spend the night with him beneath the stars. Why, oh why, hadn't she ignored the stupid prophecy and just trusted her feelings? The way things stood between them now it felt as if all her chances had been well and truly wasted.

'Don't make the same mistake Luke and I did,' Trinity told her. 'We both fell in love with people when we thought we were too young, and walked away from the loves of our lives. With Luke, for the first time I thought I could let go of the past but he's still hung up on the one that got away. If you really like this Craig, you must follow your heart.'

'Will you follow yours?' Libby asked and Trinity sighed heavily.

'No. Because I know Luke can never really be mine,' she said eventually. 'Fate's loaned him to me for a while and I have to live with that the best I can. But as for you and that delectable young kick boxer – well, I think that's something else again. In fact, he was talking about you only a few days ago. He said—'

But infuriatingly Libby didn't get to hear what it was Craig had said about her because they were interrupted by Luke striding in, full of excitement about a stunt that was being planned for his film.

'Babe, you look like you've been crying. What's up?' he said when he noticed Trin's panda-eye look. Tenderly he raised her chin with his forefinger and dropped a kiss on to her perfect nose. 'What's the matter, angel?'

'We've been watching *The Notebook*,' Libby

improvised wildly. 'And we've been bawling our eyes out, haven't we, Trin?'

Trin shot Libby a grateful glance. 'Absolutely. I just can't stop crying.'

Luke looked surprised. 'I thought you hated all that sentimental stuff, babe? You normally prefer a good old sci-fi like me. There's nothing that beats *Star Trek*, is what you always say. Now if you were crying about that bit in *The Wrath of Khan* where poor Chekov has a creature put in his ear then I could understand your tears. That's really nasty!'

Libby groaned. 'Please, Luke, no, not *Star Trek* again!'

But Trinity had perked up visibly. 'Great idea. Pop a movie on, sweetie. I could do with cheering up.'

Luke, as always when it came to his beloved *Star Trek*, didn't need asking twice and moments later he was rummaging around in a black holdall and sifting through his collection of movies.

'Can we watch the one with the whales? That's my favourite!' Trin was asking, her eyes shining and her upset forgotten. Wow! She was either a way, way better actress than anyone had ever realised, or – and this was much weirder – Trinity really was a genuine Trekkie.

Or rather, Trekker!

' 'Course we can, hon,' Luke said cheerfully. 'I love that bit when Spock goes swimming in the dolphin tank, don't you?'

'Love it!' Trin clapped her hands together. 'And then he mind melds with a whale.'

OK. It was official. These guys were nuts.

'These films come everywhere with me,' Luke explained, seeing Libby's stunned expression when he laid twenty or so DVDs on the bed. 'I always need a bit of *Star Trek* to unwind. Trin loves it, too. In fact, it was one of the first things we hand in common. It's our special unique bond.'

Libby almost laughed out loud. So it was *Star Trek* that Luke had alluded to when he said they'd bonded over a shared interest. She wasn't sure if this was better or worse than some dodgy sexual deviation.

Leaving Trin and Luke cuddled up on the bed watching Kirk and Spock save the universe for the umpteenth time, Libby borrowed some clothes from Trin and headed back into the grounds. She never thought she'd have said it but she was going to take Trinity's advice, no matter how much the thought scared her or how likely it was that she'd be rejected. And if she was now more shaky with nerves than she ever was before doing a forward-facing rappel then it was only to be expected because this was something far more terrifying.

Libby was going to find Craig and tell him *exactly* how she felt about him.

Libby threaded her way through the lush tropical gardens towards the bar. White fairy lights were strung through the trees and their light spilled into the waters of the fountains and pools which dotted the grounds. The hotel bar was situated in an elaborate Thai-style pergola, richly painted in crimsons and greens and lovingly decorated with gold swirls and dragons. But Libby didn't have time to admire the opulent surroundings. She was far too busy scanning the scene for that one dearly familiar figure.

Filled with a sudden surge of nervous energy, she ran up the steps to the bar and paused by the gilded entrance as she searched the crowd. Then her heart did a roly-poly when she saw that tall powerful figure leaning against the bar, his high cheek-boned face turned away from her as he chatted to the barman. Thank goodness he was still here and hadn't decided to cut his losses and leave! Somebody somewhere was smiling down on her because it seemed that she'd been given a second chance to put things right. This time she was determined not to muck it up.

She paused to gather herself together before speaking to him. At least she looked fairly presentable after raiding all Trinity's gorgeous products. Her hair fell in glossy golden waves to her shoulders and she'd borrowed a beautiful white Roberto Cavalli beach dress which made her tanned skin glow. Although her face was bare of makeup, her cheeks were pink with excitement and her nose was sprinkled with a cinnamon dusting of freckles from the relentless sun. Unused to wanting to look girly she swallowed back her nerves and tried to ignore how her heart was playing squash against her ribs.

Get a grip, Libby, she told herself sternly. It's only Craig! There's nothing to be nervous about.

'Is that your new little friend?' asked a mocking voice just behind her. 'You don't hang about, do you?'

Spinning round, Libby saw Hilary standing just behind her. The older girl's mouth was curled into a jeer and her eyes glittered with malice.

'Honestly, Libby,' she sneered. 'What a greedy girl you are. Isn't one man enough?'

'What?' Libby was taken aback. Somehow she'd expected that Hilary would be so embarrassed by her shameless underhand stealing of the extras that she'd be laying low somewhere. She certainly hadn't expected to bump into her in the hotel bar!

Hilary jerked her head in Craig's direction. 'I saw you with him earlier. Don't look so innocent. You were on the beach together. Tut, tut! What will Tom say? And Kyle?'

Libby flushed. 'I'm not with Tom any more, and I was certainly never with Kyle. I've no idea why Janine thinks I could have been. She's my friend.'

Hilary raised an over-plucked eyebrow. 'She probably thinks that if you could steal one girl's partner what would stop you doing the same to another, friend or not. And of course there are enough of us who've seen you creeping around with Kyle to start feeling rather suspicious.'

Libby stared at Hilary in horror. 'You told Janine I was seeing Kyle! You've convinced her it's true! For God's sake, Hilly, that's not funny. Jan's pregnant!'

She shrugged. 'I don't see anyone laughing. And you're the only one who says nothing happened with Kyle. You were happy enough to go behind my back with Tom.'

The expression on Hilary's face was so vindictive that Libby's skin prickled with unease.

'Hilly, I swear I had absolutely no idea Tom was seeing you as well. The first I knew of it was that night in Hua Hin. He's played us both for fools.'

'That's your story,' snarled Hilary.

Libby was exasperated. 'You can't seriously believe that! If you remember, you broke the news to me. I was totally shocked to learn you were with Tom. I bet he spun you that line about having to keep working life and personal lives separate, didn't he?'

Hilary tried to hide the recognition that flickered over her face. Obviously Tom had done just that.

'It should be him you're mad at, not me. And anyway, you're being ridiculous. You can't steal people!'

'Oh, can't you?' Hilary's thin lips curved into a nasty smile. 'We'll see about that.'

Libby was about to ask her what on earth she was on about when she was distracted by the sight of Craig turning from the bar and heading in their direction. His bright, unwavering gaze met hers. He was holding two glasses and a bottle of wine and Libby looked around to see if anyone else from *The Indian Prince and I* had appeared to join him. Nope; Trin and Luke were still on board the starship *Enterprise* and Eastwood Jones was nowhere in sight. Her stomach did a cartwheel of nervous excitement. He must have hoped she would show up eventually. He'd believed in her enough to know that she would overcome all her silly doubts and fears and seek him out.

Forgetting Hilary, Libby smiled up at Craig, her spirits lifting. In the soft beam of the twinkling fairy lights his hair glinted like newly minted coins and those thickly lashed deep jade eyes glittered. Wow. Why had it taken her so long to see just how incredible he was? She really, really liked this guy. Enough to finally admit her feelings for him, not just to Craig but also to herself.

'Hey,' she said softly. 'I've been looking for you.'

'Really?' Craig's gaze slid away. 'Well, I'm kind of busy at the moment, Lib.'

Reaching across her, he passed one of the wine glasses over to Hilary whose thin fingers curled tightly around the stem.

'Thanks, Craig,' she said, smiling coyly up at him from under her lashes.

Libby's chin was practically on the pink marble floor. What on earth was going on? How come Hilary was doing Trinity's shy Princess Diana thing to Craig? The woman was normally as shy as Alan Sugar on a grumpy day!

'Do you two know each other?' she asked.

'We met in the bar earlier on,' simpered Hilary, slipping her free hand into the crook of Craig's arm. 'We were both alone and abandoned so we got talking.'

Libby was thunderstruck. *Of all the scheming, conniving cows!* Hilary had seen her rowing with Craig earlier and then deliberately made a beeline for him. If she hadn't already had a grudge against the older woman for stealing the extras then she certainly had one now!

'Hilary's working on *Bridge Over the River*,' Craig said and his voice was cool. 'But then you've probably figured that out.'

'We've got so much in common,' simpered Hilary, dimpling up at Craig so sweetly that Libby felt sick.

'I got Chardonnay; I hope that's all right with you?' he said to Hilary, ignoring Libby as he smiled at her rival. 'I'm normally a tinnies man.'

'It's perfect,' breathed Hilary, sounding like a North London Marilyn Monroe. 'Just like you.'

Libby almost puked. Surely Craig was going to see through this utter guff? But to her surprise he laughed and sloshed some wine into Hilary's glass, seeming to enjoy her admiration and flattery.

'Craig, can we speak somewhere? In private?' she said, hating the fact that Hilary was sneering at her. 'There's something I really need to discuss with you.'

'Not now, Libby,' Craig said coldly. 'I'm off duty. I think you've had more than your fair share of my time.'

Stung by the ice in his tone, Libby stammered, 'There's just some film stuff I needed to run by you.' She cringed at the lie she was telling. But desperate situations call for desperate measures.

'Well, save it for tomorrow. Anyway, I'm not even

sure I'm going to be working on *The Indian Prince* for much longer.'

'What?' Stunned, Libby could only stare at him in disbelief. 'But why?'

Craig shrugged. 'I thought that was obvious? You've lost your extras. The film's way over budget and could be pulled at any minute. And maybe I just feel like a change? Hilary's offered me a non-speaking part in *Bridge Over the River* and I'm up for a new challenge.' His eyes finally met hers and she flinched at their coldness. 'I'm through with the old game. In fact, I'm bored.'

'He'll be a fantastic actor,' gushed Hilary. 'Don't you think so?'

'Sure,' Libby said, feeling lost. She tried to catch Craig's eye but he was studiously avoiding her.

'See you later then,' Hilly said airily. Then she and Craig were walking away from her out into the star-sprinkled night. One of Craig's strong tanned hands rested in the small of Hilary's back. As Libby stared, the older woman glanced back over her shoulder and gave her a wide, gloating smile.

Libby sagged against the gilded balustrade. Hilary was punishing her for all the trouble with Tom by deliberately making a play for Craig. And because she'd hurt and rejected Craig one time too many he was only too happy to let her flatter his ego. She'd never slept with Luke either and now Craig was punishing her for something she'd never done. Thanks a lot, stars!

Hilary had won. And Libby had most definitely lost.

Her vision blurring with tears Libby stumbled out into the velvet night. She didn't want to stay in the bar and she couldn't bear to join Luke and Trin for their *Star Trek* marathon. Slowly and sadly she made her way through the garden and down to the infinity pool where she kicked off Trin's glittery sandals and dipped her toes into the cool dark water. Then, and only then, when she was sure that she was alone and unseen, Libby let the tears slip silently down her cheeks.

Angela had warned Libby about being a danger to men. What she'd forgotten to point out was that one man would prove to be an even greater danger to her.

And right now she wasn't sure quite how she was going to survive.

'Oh. My. God. I simply can't believe you're asking me to give my extras back. Darling, it's an impossibility! Look around you! We are like, *so*, not doing that right now.'

Fabian, the director of *Bridge Over the River*, rolled his eyes and tossed his gleaming mane of chestnut hair. In spite of the sweltering heat he was wearing a crimson crushed-velvet frock coat and frilly shirt. His only concession to the sweltering temperature was a large feather fan which he flapped around his face. Although in the middle of serious negotiations to win their extras back – a mission on which rested her future career as a casting agent – Libby couldn't help smiling. Fabian was the exact opposite of what you'd expect from the director of a high-octane action movie. He was a dead ringer for Gok Wan and she half expected him to start sizing up her bangers and flourishing control knickers at any minute.

Talk about prisoner of war camp!

After a long night spent on Luke's vast sofa, a night where she'd cried so much that she'd almost been in danger of drowning, Libby was now on set and frantic to secure the return of her extras. So far her morning was proving to be every bit as rubbish as the previous evening had been. Although the pale and slender Fabian looked as though a puff of the wind machine could blow him over, he was proving to be very determined when it came to hanging on to his extras. Nothing either Tom or Libby had said would change his mind and the amount of money she was going to have to offer the extras made her feel queasy.

'Listen, you!' roared Eastwood Jones, whose face was even redder than Fabian's jacket. 'Those are *my* extras. You've stolen them and I want them back, now!'

'Ooo! Mardy!' trilled Fabian. 'Listen, angel, those divine boys are working for me now. Why don't you do us all a favour and toddle off, will you?'

Eastwood's fists were clenched in rage and he was practically breathing fire while mouthing wordlessly. Libby couldn't help thinking whoever chose these two directors for their respective movies had got them the wrong way around. Fabian would be much more at home with *The Indian Prince and I* whereas Eastwood would be in his element with a big-budget action movie like this. Maybe they could solve this whole mess by switching over?

'We cast those extras first,' Tom pointed out. 'Without them we are going to have major problems. It's hardly fair play to steal them.'

Fabian shrugged. 'Darling boy, all's fair in love and movies! And surely you can see that they're a tad busy? We're practically ready to shoot.' He flapped a languid pale hand in the direction of the set where a scene was being prepped. It was certainly elaborate: a rope bridge strung across a ravine with people clinging to it. She could understand why Fabian wasn't prepared to listen.

But Eastwood exploded at this sight. 'Those are my extras! If you don't return them I'll bloody well fetch them back myself!'

'You will not,' Fabian told him and suddenly there was steel beneath the flamboyant exterior. 'They've made their decision and they want to work for me. How dare you come storming on to *my* set making threats? I'll call security and have you thrown out.'

'It'll be the last thing you ever do!' blustered Eastwood, but the colour had drained from his face and Libby could tell he was worried. Without the extras he knew his own film was doomed and Fabian knew it, too.

'Look, let's settle this once and for all,' Fabian suggested, prepared to be reasonable because he knew he held all the cards. Turning away from them he murmured something into a walkie-talkie and moments later Hilary was striding towards them with a big folder tucked under her arm.

Libby heard Tom inhale sharply. Libby's skin was bristling and she found that she was scrutinising her closely for any slight sign that she may have shared more than just a glass of wine with Craig. She certainly looked more full of beans than Heinz, her shiny bob swinging in time with each step and her usually pale skin tanned light gold. There was a secretive smile playing around her narrow lips and seeing it, Libby's heart lurched. Was Hilary smiling at some memory of what had passed between her and Craig? Was she planning to meet up with him later on? These thoughts burned like acid and Libby shook them away impatiently. She needed to get a grip. All that really mattered right now was saving the film. The personal stuff would have to wait.

'Is there a problem, Fabbie?' Hilary asked innocently. Her cold eyes swept over Libby and her mouth curved into a smirk. 'Not this thing with the extras again?'

'Darling, it's such a tiresome bore but Eastwood seems to think that all your lovely extras were actually contracted to him first.' Fabian yawned theatrically. 'Tell me it isn't so?'

Hilary's over-plucked eyebrows shot into her fringe

and her eyes widened with mock horror.

'I had no idea that you'd got these guys to sign contracts!' she gasped, flipping open her big folder to a section marked in blood red with the fatal words CONTRACTS FOR EXTRAS. 'I guess if they've signed with you first, Libby, then these are null and void. You *did* get them to sign contracts, didn't you?'

Suddenly the blood drained from Libby's head with a woosh. Hilary's eyes were gleaming with triumph and Fabian stared at her questioningly.

'Did they sign with you first?'

Libby's face was on fire. 'No,' she whispered.

'What!' Eastwood turned on her and his roar of wrath was so loud that her hair was blown back from her face. 'Tell me you're kidding! Of course you got them to sign contracts. You're not that bloody stupid.'

Libby had the hideous sensation that she was hurtling down a helter-skelter at top speed. Whizzing past her and left behind for ever were the film, her career, and any hope she might have of sorting things out with Craig. Because of her incompetence everything was ruined!

'It's not something I've ever had to do before,' she stuttered.

'How could you be so bloody stupid?' Eastwood raged, his eyes bulging and his face purple.

'Don't blame Libby; it's my job to work the

contracts out,' Tom said, stepping forward and putting an arm around Libby's shaking shoulders. 'I was ill which was why she had to handle everything herself. She did a great job, considering. And nobody could have guessed in a million years that another casting agent would stoop so low as to poach forty extras from a fellow professional.'

'Your whole firm is a disgrace!' stormed Eastwood, rounding on Tom and raising a clenched fist to hit him. To his credit, Tom stood his ground, although beneath his lawn shirt Libby could feel his heartbeat start to race.

'I'm sorry,' she choked, close to tears – it was a miracle in itself that she had any left after last night's deluge.

'Fuck *sorry*!' the director swore. 'Your mistake has cost tens of millions and screwed up the entire project. You'll be more than sorry when I make sure nobody in the industry ever hires your excuse for a casting company again!'

And spinning on his jack-booted heel he stalked off yelling for his private jet to be made ready and for somebody to fetch Trinity. Libby and Tom, it seemed, could make their own way back.

'Ooo, get him,' remarked Fabian. 'What a temper!'

Libby gulped. She didn't blame Eastwood Jones at all for being incandescent with rage. He was totally in the right, wasn't he? Never mind the fact that Tom had been ill and Kyle had decided not to show up for work, it was her oversight that had cost them everything. She was a danger to everything.

'We'll sort this, Libby, I promise,' Tom said, squeezing her shoulder sympathetically. 'You know how volatile Eastwood is. He'll calm down in a minute, you'll see.'

'You should have stuck with me, sweetheart,' Hilary told him triumphantly. 'I never would have made such a stupid mistake. But if you must hang out with inexperienced kids . . .' Her words faded away but her broad gloating smile remained, and Libby couldn't blame her. Hilly was a bitch but, however unwittingly, Libby had hurt her as much as one woman can hurt another. The agony she'd suffered last night as she'd imagined Hilary and Craig together had been unbearable and nothing had ever really happened between her and Craig. How much worse must it have been for Hilary to discover that the man she loved was cheating on her?

Talk about karma coming back to bite you on the bum . . .

With a strangled sob, Libby shook off Tom's hand and tore away. But it didn't matter how far she ran, Hilly's triumphant smile still hung before her like the Cheshire Cat's. Taking refuge behind a trailer she closed her eyes and groaned. What could she do to put things right? Except find a few million to save the film, of course, which was easier said than done when even NatWest wouldn't extend her overdraft.

'You run from the legions of hell but they will always chase you,' remarked Panom, strolling over and crouching into the lotus position beside her.

Today the old man looked rested, as well he might after sleeping in a ten-thousand-dollar-a-night suite. But his eyes were filled with concern. 'Running will only make your demons hurry.'

Libby groaned. 'Let me guess? *Buddhist Assassin* again?'

Panom inclined his head. 'Is very good film. Much truth. You should watch.'

'Do you know what? I think I will. Seeing as I'm unemployed I'll have enough time to watch the whole trilogy and the extended scenes.'

'Unemployed?' Panom echoed. 'What happen, little one? You find extras! Surely much joy?'

'Sadly not,' said Libby grimly before going on to tell him the whole sorry tale. 'So no film and no job. It's all over. And please,' she added seeing Panom open his mouth to speak, 'don't quote from that flipping movie again. I might just have to leap into the river and drown myself.'

'As you wish,' said Panom graciously. Together they

sat in silence for a while and watched the hustle and bustle of the film crew carry on around them. Libby felt a beachball-sized lump swell in her throat because she'd loved being a part of this world, had really thought that her future lay in casting movies. Now she supposed it would be back to waiting tables and trying to figure out what to do next. Not a great prospect at the grand old age of twenty-four.

'So film stop. Craig now working on other film?' Panom asked eventually.

Ripping her thoughts away from the unhappy image of herself asking customers whether they wanted to make their meals *go large*, Libby stared at Panom.

'Craig's really working on the other film.' She sighed. It was inevitable really, especially now he was with Hilary. 'I suppose they need as many extras as they can get.'

But Panom's crinkly face was puzzled. 'No, little one. Craig not extra. Craig is stunt man. He doing big big stunt today for Mr Scottman. On bridge!'

Libby goggled at him. 'You're seriously telling me that Hilary's hired Craig as Luke's stunt double? That's impossible. Craig isn't trained.'

But Panom was most insistent, having apparently been told exactly this by Craig himself, who was over the moon about it. *He would be*, thought Libby in panic as she sprinted back to find Hilary. This was just the kind of daredevil activity which was the breath of life to Craig. What he didn't realise was that these kinds of film stunts required more than guts and sheer nerve; they needed years of training and skill to pull off. What the hell was Hilary thinking to place Craig in such danger rather than using a professional stuntman? She knew there were rules to protect the extras and keep them safe.

Her mouth dry with fear for Craig, Libby knew she had to say something before it was too late.

But back at the set Hilary was far too preoccupied by having the mother of all rows with Tom to be interested in listening to anything Libby might have to say.

'All this talk of contracts is rich coming from you!' Tom was yelling. 'You're the one in breach of contract! You're signed to Cast Away, remember? You can't even think about working for somebody else until you've worked out your notice for me.'

'So sue me, asshole!' shrieked Hilary, her face twisted with rage.

'Oh, I will, don't worry,' Tom yelled back. 'Unless you rip up those contracts I'll sue you to kingdom come! Then you'll be sorry. You work for me, dammit!'

'What a shame you didn't think about that when you were busy screwing Libby!' Hilary hissed back.

'You're such a child, Tom. You couldn't handle how serious things were with us so you had to screw it up by shagging the youngest thing in the office. And now you have the nerve to be angry because she isn't as good at the work as me! Make your mind up. What do you really want?'

Charming, thought Libby. But unpleasant as all this was to hear she couldn't help feeling that there was an element of truth in what Hilary was saying. When she searched her heart she knew that an escape from responsibilities was exactly what Tom had enjoyed about their carefree, no-strings relationship. It was when she had wanted to get serious that he'd started to back off. Adult life and commitment weren't particularly high up on his list of priorities.

Whereas Craig was right at the top of hers, and she needed to shut this squabbling pair up so she could find out exactly what Hilary was thinking of by placing him in such danger.

'For God's sake, grow up both of you!'

Fed up with listening to their constant rowing, Libby strode in-between them. Both Tom and Hilary stopped in midflow.

'You guys obviously still have feelings for each other,' she continued swiftly. 'Hilly, you wouldn't want revenge so much if you didn't still care about Tom. And Tom, you're mad with Hilly because you're angry with yourself for cocking it all up. You're crazy about each other, and you're both terrified by that.'

Hilary and Tom stared at her with open mouths.

'Just face the facts: you're meant for each other,' she flared. 'Tom, you never felt anything real for me; you were just trying to pretend that you were in your twenties again. And let's face it, that was never going to work. You've no idea who N-Dubz are, for a start!

'And, Hilly, you've more than proved that you're the best casting agent around. Tom would have to be mental not to know that already. Cast Away really can't run without you. And Tom certainly can't. He took to his bed for days when you left.' Because of the food poisoning, but Hilary didn't need to know that.

Hilary looked at Tom. 'Is that true?'

'It's true,' Tom said slowly, looking at Libby, who nodded at him encouragingly before turning back to Hilary. 'God, I've been such an idiot, Hilly. I love you so much. Please come back. I need you.'

Hilary swallowed. 'For what it's worth, I've really missed you. I guess that means that in spite of every-thing I still love you too, even if I can't quite forgive you.'

Then they were in each other's arms, crying and laughing and kissing. Libby almost expected a string orchestra to strike up some big romantic number while the sun decided to set ten hours early. At least somebody had got their happy ending.

A sharp tugging of her sleeve alerted Libby to Panom who had joined them. His lined face clouded with worry as he cried, 'Little one, look! Look! See? On bridge?'

Now that she was no longer preoccupied with stopping World War Three breaking out, Libby saw that the film set below was teeming with people running backwards and forwards like disturbed ants while Fabian was shouting into his megaphone. All eyes though were not on the director, as might be expected during such a large-scale scene.

Instead, everyone's attention was focused on the bridge where a stuntman was dangling one hundred feet above the river, his foot trapped in a harness and with nothing to break the fall into the water below. Libby cried out in terror. A drop from such a height was akin to hitting a concrete floor and would mean instant death. As the man struggled to free himself it was clear to see that the harness was growing looser with every desperate twist he made, leaving him only minutes from certain disaster.

Libby's hands flew to her mouth in horror. There was no mistaking those long corkscrew blond curls.

The man trapped in the harness was Craig.

23

Libby was running down past the cameras and
props and on to the set before her brain had
registered what she was doing. All she knew was that
she had to act fast. Craig only had minutes before the
buckle on that harness bent out of shape and his foot
slipped. She had to do something!

Staring about her wildly Libby spotted a crane that
housed one of the cameras for high-angled shots. To
the left of this was a series of coiled bungee ropes.
OK, so she had a crane, she had some ropes and
standing on the set she even had forty young fit extras.
Maybe, just maybe . . .

Calling Panom over, Libby quickly explained her
plan. The old man listened and nodded rather than
trying to dissuade her or weave in some of his favourite
movie lines. Then he was repeating her idea in rapid
Thai to the extras and film crew who were nodding and
gasping in mingled awe and horror.

'They think too dangerous,' he told her. 'They say

very crazy girl. Lee say he go instead of you.'

But Libby was already coiling a rope around her waist, using the intricate knots that she'd learned last year while climbing Kilimanjaro. Knots she knew would hold when tested by the weight of a human body.

'Lee doesn't have my experience,' she told him. 'Besides, he needs to be in a boat to pick us up if – I mean *when* – this works. Now go and tell him to find a boat! Leave the bungee jumping to me.'

Once satisfied with her ropes, Libby beckoned over four of the burliest extras and seconds later they were right behind her as she scaled the crane. Sweat ran down her face and her breath caught in her lungs but still Libby continued to climb. Once she stood on the top of the crane looking over the edge, the familiar surge of adrenalin washed over her and her limbs tingled with stomach-churning excitement. Never before had she needed to be so brave or so accurate: she was only going to get one shot at this and everything that mattered in the world depended on getting it right. If she miscalculated then she and Craig were both dead.

For a split second she stood poised on the precipice. The ropes behind her were slack but the four men who held them looked grimly determined. Libby knew that as dangerous as this makeshift bungee was, she had to trust them to hold her. At ten stone she was far from heavy but she knew from experience that when her body mass reached the end of the rope the jolt on the upper end would be enormous. Usually when bungee jumping, she would work out the exact tension of the cords based on her height and weight but this time it was just a case of grabbing the nearest rope to hand. She only prayed that this one was in good condition and could stretch far enough for what she had in mind.

What was it the psychic back in Hua Hin had said? Something about not getting tied up in knots? The irony of this wasn't lost on Libby. But what choice did she have? Craig's life depended on this. Besides, her days of listening to flaky psychics were over. From now on she was done with her silly dependence on astrology.

Libby launched herself into the air and instantly had the sensation of weightlessness as the world flew by in a blur. Then the ropes snapped taut, pulling against her waist so sharply that for a few moments she gasped for breath.

She glided up and down before the elastic of the rope came to a halt.

And, amazingly, her crazy, stupid, risky idea had worked! She was now dangling at the same height as Craig and there wasn't a moment to lose.

'Boy, am I glad to see you!' he said, trying to make light of the situation but with terror etched on his face.

'You need to do everything I tell you,' she ordered and he nodded back.

She glanced down at the silver-ribbon river and her stomach cartwheeled. This was so dangerous. One wrong move and he would plummet into the water far below. Cold sweat broke out between her shoulder blades and her mouth dried. Oh, God. She had to get this right. She couldn't fail Craig now.

The wooden bridge creaked. It had been designed to be blown up; it wasn't as sturdy as it could have been. But, giving a thumbs up to the guys above, Libby swung back and forth on the end of the rope while the camera crew manoeuvred the crane closer and closer to Craig.

'Up a bit!' she shouted down to Panom, who shouted in Thai the instructions to the men.

Craig kept quiet but, as the wooden beams gave another worrying creak, he looked up in alarm.

'Now left, just a half a metre!' she yelled.

Through a series of complicated leveraging and adjustments they were able to bring her parallel to the exact spot where Craig was still suspended in his rapidly loosening harness.

He was just a fingernail's reach away. One more swing and she'd be there.

Straining every single muscle she stretched out her arm. Her hand closed round the top of his harness and their bodies bumped together. Even a hundred feet up in the air and taut with terror she felt a fizz of excitement. *Focus, Libby! Focus!*

Craig clung on tight to Libby and they hugged, partly because her rope was his lifeline, but partly because Libby was so relieved to finally have him in her arms.

'G'day,' Libby said.

'Libby?' Craig was so white that his eyes burned fever bright against his skin. Sweat from the exertion of trying to stay still while his harness gave way had dampened his curls to tight springs and the tautness of his mouth spoke volumes about his exhaustion. 'This is crazy. You're taking far too much of a risk!'

They both looked down at the churning waters below. Then the harness gave again and Craig cried out as he dropped another few metres, taking Libby with him.

'Let go!' he ordered. 'I'm not having you hurt because of me. No way!'

She shook her head. 'I'm not leaving you.'

'Seriously, Lib, go back. I'm only seconds away from falling and if you don't let go, you'll go with me and I can't bear that.'

'I'm *not* leaving you,' Libby told him again. 'You

promised to do everything I say, so hold still. I'm going to get in the right position then tie you to me.'

Craig groaned. 'It's too dangerous!'

For a second her blue eyes held his. 'Losing you is far more dangerous,' she said. 'If anything happened to you . . .' Her words faded because they were still a hundred feet above the glinting river, still in terrible danger. All the things she longed to say to him would have to wait.

'Hold still, I need to let go. But I'm coming right back. I just need to swing closer for a better grip,' she told him. 'When I do, you have to hold on to me as tightly as you can. That's the only way I can stay still long enough to knot the ropes around your waist before you kick your foot out of the harness. Do you understand?'

His wide eyes met hers and even in this extreme danger her heart gave a leap to see the intensity of feeling that dwelt there.

'Put my arms around you and hold you tight,' he repeated. 'I will.'

Somehow, and she would never know quite how she managed it, Libby let go of him, then swung her body across the chasm between them until she felt Craig's strong arms close around her and pull her tight. His grip was more sure than a moment ago. Her heart was hammering against her ribs when she felt his harness give again.

Hurry, she told herself. *There isn't much time!*

As fast as she could, Libby lashed the free end of her makeshift harness around Craig's waist, pulling the knots tight just as her climbing instructor had taught her. Then she slipped Craig's foot free from his own tangled harness and held her breath for the moment of truth: if her handiwork was anything less than perfect then they would plummet into the river! Her throat dry with fear she prayed that the knots wouldn't slip. There was no going back now. If she'd got this wrong then they would both tumble to a watery grave.

But Libby's climbing instructor had done her proud. The knots held fast. Craig was safely in her arms.

'You little beaut, you did it!' yelled Craig, cupping her face between his strong hands and kissing her soundly while they were gently lowered into the water. 'You did it!'

Then they were underwater and he was kissing her nose, her eyelids and her lips over and over again as he was caught up in the sheer relief of being alive. Weak with joy she let him kiss her, knowing that this wasn't really genuine emotion but the euphoria that always followed a particularly dangerous jump. Libby felt exactly the same way except for one pretty significant detail – her feelings for Craig were one hundred per cent real. She wanted nothing more than to kiss him back and thread her fingers through his glorious hair and feel that golden stubble rasp against her cheeks, but she knew she had to be cautious. After all, less than twenty-four hours ago he'd been with Hilary.

The cold waters of the river distracted Craig and coughing and spluttering he and Libby had to wait for a moment while Lee and Panom located them.

Moments later Libby and Craig were sprawled on the deck while Lee unfastened the ropes and Panom wept in relief. Libby knew exactly how he felt. When Craig wrapped his arms around her and pulled her close she didn't resist but instead laid her head against his chest and closed her eyes. They were both safe and unharmed and for now, at least, nothing mattered more than this.

'I don't believe it! You're back – and with the extras! How on earth did you ever manage that?'

Kyle's amazed expression as Libby, Craig, Tom, Hilary and the forty extras strolled on to the set of *The Indian Prince and I* was an absolute picture. Libby was almost equally amazed to find him still in Hua Hin after his vanishing act of a few days earlier, and was even more surprised to see that he was holding the hand of a radiant Janine who was beaming at her.

'Just how long have you got?' Tom asked him with a

grin. 'Or shall we just put it down to the fact that I'm a genius?'

Catching Craig's wink, Libby laughed to herself. Tom could believe this if he wanted to but she knew the true story. Following Craig's near catastrophe, a choked Hilary had confessed that she hadn't intended to actually use him as a stuntman but had only said it to keep Craig on the set and wind Libby up. Nothing had happened between her and Craig, Hilary had insisted, her eyes pleading with Tom as she said this; she'd just wanted to get even. There was no way Craig should really have been allowed on set, but she'd forgotten to tell him it was all a wind-up.

After this, things had got rather ugly: a furious Fabian sacked Hilary on the spot and Craig threatened to sue the production company of *Bridge Over the River*. The only thing that might persuade him not to do so, he'd told Fabian thoughtfully, was if the forty extras were released from their contracts and allowed to return to Hua Hin. Gnashing his teeth in rage, Fabian hadn't really had any choice but to let them go. And when the extras discovered they would now get twice as much money they couldn't leave quickly enough!

'Brag all you like,' Kyle told Tom. 'My competitive days are over. The only thing I'm worrying about from now on is my family.' As he said this he pulled Janine close and dropped a tender kiss on to the crown of her head. *Phew*, thought Libby, *thank goodness those two have sorted out their differences!*

Janine stepped forward and took Libby's hands in hers. 'I'm so sorry, Libby. I've been so stupid. I know that nothing went on between you and Kyle. I think my hormones got the better of me.'

'My recreational drug habit and secret smoking probably didn't help,' Kyle admitted. 'Time for me to grow up now I'm going to be a dad, I guess.'

'Hey! What's this?' As she held Janine's small hand Libby felt something cold and hard graze her palm. Uncoiling their hands she saw a perfect diamond solitaire nestled on Janine's engagement finger. Libby's eyes widened. 'Babe! Is that what I think it is?'

Janine laughed. 'Yep! Kyle's proposed and we're going to get married as soon as we're back home. We're having our honeymoon now which is a bit topsy turvy, I suppose, but we've never done things the conventional way.'

At this point there was much hugging and kissing and Tom called for champagne which Janine pointed out was rather a waste since she couldn't drink!

'Well, maybe Hilly and I would like a glass to celebrate?' Tom protested, his arm slung around his girlfriend's bony shoulders. 'We're officially back together, too.'

'They were never officially together in the first place as I recall,' Kyle whispered in Libby's ear. 'Wasn't that the whole problem?'

'Ssh!' She nudged him in the ribs. 'Let's just be happy for them.'

Kyle's merry freckled face broke into a smile. 'I'm all for being happy, especially now we've got our extras back. Eastwood will be thrilled. He's been in a right mood since he flew back. I was amazed he chartered a plane for you.'

'He needed those extras,' Libby said cheerfully as Kyle led the way to the set. 'I'm sure he'd have been more than happy for me and Craig to crawl back through the jungle no matter what injuries we may have. And talking of injuries, how's Dash doing?'

'He'll live,' Kyle told her. 'It turns out that our drama queen Dash only broke a fingernail. The show will go on!'

Libby felt about twenty stone lighter with the relief of hearing all this. It seemed that the curse was lifting with every step she took! Kyle's relationship was back on track and Dash wasn't really injured at all. Heck, she'd even saved Craig's life! Maybe everything was going to work out after all?

The latest scene was being shot down on the icing-sugar sands of Hua Hin beach. It was a scene set in the harem and Libby instantly recognised it as the one where Dash's Indian prince showed his love for Trin's character by washing her feet.

'Action!' hollered Eastwood from his perch aboard a dolly, and instantly the set came to life. Libby shivered. No matter how many times she saw a take, the magic of the story never ceased to amaze her.

Trinity appeared in the arched doorway of the harem set, pausing for a moment and ensuring that all eyes were drawn to her perfect body and blond hair rippling to her supple waist, about which a jewelled girdle fastened her gown of translucent peach silk. Then, every inch the pampered queen, she stalked across the set followed by a retinue of slaves. The fat chief eunuch came first, then six really fit black guys with the most amazing abs Libby had ever seen and finally the harem slaves.

Wait a minute! That older woman at the back of the scene looked familiar. Squinting against the glare of the lights Libby peered closer and shook her head in disbelief when she saw that the hotel psychic was part of the scene. She was an actor!

'Cut!' boomed Eastwood and the church-like silence was replaced by chatter and a ripple of applause.

'Who's that woman?' Libby asked Janine, pointing to her so-called psychic.

'That's Ella Evans. You must have come across her before?' Janine looked surprised. 'She's one of the best method actors out. She's never made it big but I think she makes a pretty good living doing bit parts.'

Libby laughed out loud. Hadn't she given Ella Evans $300 only a few days ago? Yep, she would say that wasn't doing too badly for ten minutes of acting the part of a psychic. And she'd fallen for it hook, line and sinker. It had all been total nonsense! The prophecy – *you'll be a danger to many men* – was just nonsense, too. Of course that was all it was!

A commotion from on set drew her attention back to the present. Dash had thrown the silver bowl of water across the room and was complaining loudly while Trin screamed at him.

'I should have a double to do this!' Dash whined, with a toss of his dark curls. 'This is disgusting. Surely washing feet counts as manual labour and my contract stipulates no manual labour. I'm a film star, not a podiatrist!'

Libby's eyes widened. How come she'd never noticed as a teen that Dash's mouth had a really petulant set to it? Eastwood was going to go nuts at such a display of diva-ish behaviour.

But weirdly, Eastwood didn't do his usual entire Guy Fawkes Day's worth of fireworks act. Instead he clambered from his camera perch and crouched down beside Dash to listen to his complaint, placing a tender hand on Dash's knee and soothing him. Only somebody watching closely would have noticed the look that passed between the two men and Libby could hardly believe her eyes.

Eastwood's face was so filled with love that he no longer looked like Shrek's uglier brother but almost sweet and gentle. Dash must have confessed his feelings after all – and Eastwood felt the same way! How unbelievable was that? If fate did exist – and the jury was still out as far as Libby was now concerned – it was certainly on her side.

'Libby, you're back!' called Trin, waving across the set at her. 'What did you do with those sandals I lent you? They're Manolo, you know?'

Actually Libby didn't know; she wouldn't recognise a designer shoe if one came stomping up and kicked her in the bum, but she never got to answer anyway because with a roar of delight Eastwood came charging over, scattering cast and crew as he did so, like a rhino dressed in Bermuda shorts.

'God damn! You did it! You really did it!' he boomed, crushing Libby in such a tight bear hug that her limbs feared for their lives.

'Not just me,' Libby squeaked once he'd released her and she'd got her breath back. 'Craig and Panom helped too. I couldn't have found the extras without them. And if it weren't for Craig then Fabian would have never released the extras.'

'Well, however you did it I'm helluva grateful,' the director said. 'Anything you want, girly, you just say so and it's yours. New car? Posh frock? Date with Orlando Bloom?'

Ooh! That was an idea, and if she weren't so head-over-heels crazy about Craig, Libby might have been sorely tempted. But there was nothing she wanted apart from Craig to forgive her. Powerful as Eastwood Jones was, Libby didn't think even he could manage that. However, there was something else that sprung to mind . . .

'Would you give Panom a role in the film?' She asked Eastwood. 'He's movie mad and we couldn't have done anything without his help.'

Eastwood clapped one meaty hand on her shoulder and Libby's legs nearly buckled under the sheer weight.

'Consider yourself hired!' the director told Panom, who immediately started jumping about as though his feet had grown springs. 'First thing tomorrow I want you on set. The fight scene, I think.'

'My dream it has come true!' Panom turned to Libby and his eyes were bright with tears. 'Thank you, little one! Because of you Panom will be in the movies at last.'

'But you don't get away so easily, young lady.' The director's eyes were still on Libby which, since they had all the strength of prison searchlights, was a bit disconcerting. She gulped. What was coming now? Was it the overdue bollocking about the forgotten contracts? She hung her head. If so, it was fair enough; she totally deserved it for making such a big mistake.

Eastwood Jones placed a sausagey finger under Libby's chin, tilting up her face until she was gazing into his surprisingly gentle big brown eyes.

'I've heard about what you did this morning and I'm not about to let you get away. I like someone with balls!'

Libby stifled a nervous giggle. She'd already figured that out!

'Which is why,' he continued, 'I want to offer you a permanent job working for my production company. You'll be perfect for casting stuntmen!'

She stared at him unable to quite believe it. 'You want me to work for you as a casting agent. For real?'

Jones nodded. 'For real. I'll get my people to set the paperwork in motion. Next month you're flying out to the US with me to cast my new film, *Danger Men*. No excuses. This fall, you're gonna be there!'

Having imparted this bombshell he strode back to the set leaving Libby gazing after him in disbelief. *Danger Men*? A casting agent for stuntmen and a job where she'd put men in perilous danger on a daily basis?

No. Way.

Maybe there was something to this prophecy business after all!

On the other hand, she thought, as she traced her way through the crowd and down to the shore where she could see Craig standing alone by the surf, she'd not really harmed anyone else, had she? Panom's life had been in danger when the boat sank but he was fine now and had his dream movie role. Dash hadn't been beaten to a pulp by an enraged Eastwood – quite the opposite, in fact! And as for Craig, well yes, maybe she had put him in danger, but she'd saved his life as well, hadn't she? Surely that had to mean that the universe, or at least the little bit of it that belonged to Libby Forster, was back in balance and harmony?

Craig was standing right by the shoreline, his bare feet partially buried in the soft sand, and his hair lifting gently in the warm breeze. The apricot light of the sinking sun shone down on him and turned his hair to molten gold. Watching him, Libby shivered. How weird it was that only a short while ago she hadn't known Craig even existed and now he meant everything to her. If she was going to believe in fate then this was the part that really made sense; everything in Libby told her she was destined to be with this man.

'Hey,' she said, joining him.

'Hey,' Craig replied, smiling down at her. He

reached out and laced his fingers through hers. 'You look thoughtful. What are you thinking about?'

Libby took a deep breath. This was it. Time for the truth.

'About us.'

Craig pulled her close. 'What about us?'

Those strong arms held her so close that for a moment she could hardly think straight.

'About being together,' she confessed, and her heart began to race faster than it ever did when she was out running. 'Just you and me. No Hilary, no Panom and certainly no silly prophecies.'

His arms tightened around her. 'Are you sure this is really what you want? You're not going to change your mind? Or be afraid of what that psychic said? Or run off with Luke Scottman?'

'I never slept with—'

Craig placed a finger on her lips. 'Ssh. I know. Trin explained everything. I came to find you after I had a drink with Hilary because I felt crook about treating you so badly that evening. I think she was keen to carry on with her *Star Trek* movie though, because she set me straight pretty damn fast! In fact, I thought she was going to deck me for having such slanderous thoughts about her boyfriend!'

She laughed. 'No, I think she just wanted to see Spock's mind meld with a whale!'

'What?' Craig looked so cute when confused that her heart twisted with tenderness.

'Nothing. I just think Trin knows how I feel about you.' She smiled. 'She had a go at me about wasting precious time.'

'She's right,' Craig agreed. 'I don't want to waste another minute either. Unless you've changed your mind?'

Libby shook her head. 'This is what I want. It's all I've ever wanted. I just didn't know it until now.'

'I love you, Libby,' Craig said hoarsely. 'I loved you from the moment you first stepped into my life. It was like being dazzled by the sun and I haven't been able to see anything but you ever since. It sounds crazy, I know, but I felt as though I'd met my soulmate.'

His hand strayed to her cheek, brushing a lock of hair back and caressing her soft skin. Libby had jumped from high buildings and taken a million other crazy risks but now she experienced the biggest and most thrilling adrenalin rush of them all.

'I love you, too,' she murmured. 'It's crazy and it makes no sense, but I feel exactly the same.'

The rays of the sinking sun washed over them as they held each other close and watched the water shimmer a thousand rosy hues. Libby's hands wound themselves into the soft curls at the nape of his neck as though they would never let go again. His lips strayed to the curve of her throat. That slightest of touches made her catch her breath, then Craig was kissing her and flames of pure joy made her heart race and her blood gallop through her veins. Freefall had nothing on this!

Libby's eyes closed with delight and, kissing Craig back, she suddenly knew one thing for certain: the greatest and most exciting adventure of her life was only just beginning!

Phuket – one month later

Libby yawned and stretched. What luxury to be sleeping in a bed at last rather than in a trailer or a pallet on the jungle floor! If anyone thought working in movies meant leading a glamorous lifestyle then they really ought to try working with Eastwood Jones. Apart from those five amazing days at Hua Hin the rest of the shoot had been really basic.

Still, it had all been worth it in the end. The movie was done, what she'd seen of the rushes looked amazing, and now they were in Phuket for the wrap party. After that she'd go home to England for a few weeks to show Craig off to her delighted sister and then both she and her boyfriend would be starting work on *Danger Men*. Did life really get any better than this?

Boyfriend! She rolled the word around on her

tongue, smiling because it still sounded so strange. That term didn't really sum up Craig at all! How could it? He was so much more than just a boyfriend. Best friend, running partner, colleague, diving buddy, lover . . .

At this thought Libby's smile widened and turning her head she saw that Craig was sprawled out at her side, his tanned skin honey-hued against the white sheets and his mop of golden curls fanned out across the pillow. One muscled arm was flung out above his head and even in sleep his wide generous mouth curved upwards. Sometimes Libby had to pinch herself to make sure he was real. After four weeks together her arms were so covered in bruises it looked like she was *doing* the stunts rather than choreographing them!

Reaching out, she trailed her fingers across his chest, loving the taut firmness of those sculpted muscles beneath her hand.

'Mmm,' murmured Craig, his eyes still closed, his long lashes still brushing his cheeks. 'That's a nice wake-up call.'

'It gets better,' Libby promised. Slipping her hand beneath the covers, her fingers wandered lower until they found *exactly* what they were looking for. Her eyes widened in surprise. Goodness, that was impressive for such an early start! Actually, it was a bit more than impressive. It was positively scary! And it was moving in a really weird way, all odd and bendy, a bit like a—

'Oh my God,' screamed Libby, leaping out of bed as though she'd been scalded. 'It's huge!'

'Thanks, babe.' Craig gave her a sleepy smile. 'Hey, what are you looking so worried about? Come back to bed.'

'Not on your life! Kick off the covers – now!'

'OK, bossy boots,' Craig grumbled goodnaturedly. 'If you're so keen to have a look, here we go!' And he kicked off the thin cotton sheet to reveal an enormous snake, and not one of the trouser variety!

'Jeez!' Craig was the other side of the bedroom quicker than you could say *python*. 'Stay back, Lib! That's a mean-looking bugger!'

Libby didn't need telling twice. Snatching up the sheet and winding it around her body she clambered on to a chair and watched while Craig made a dive for the intruder.

'Lucky I'm from Oz!' he said, somehow managing to scoop the snake up just below its head and tossing it through the mosquito net and out into the garden. 'We kinda grew up having to remove these little fellas from just about everywhere. And as for the funnel spiders, well they *are* nasty.'

Libby shuddered. 'Then we are definitely living in the UK!'

'Don't look so worried! He wasn't deadly, babe,' Craig assured her. 'But maybe I should've pretended it was so I can be your hero?'

Crossing the room he reached out and lifted her easily from the chair and swung her into his arms.

'Snakes in my bed,' he whispered huskily into her hair. 'Whatever next? Maybe it's true after all? You *are* a danger to men.'

His dancing eyes, the exact bluey-green hue of the sea beyond, twinkled down at her and suddenly Libby was aware that the snake was back, only this time hopefully one that wouldn't bite her! Suddenly she couldn't wait to get back under the covers.

Libby tightened her arms around his neck. 'Come back to bed and I'll show you exactly how dangerous I am!'

'I'll think I'll take you up on that,' he murmured, dropping a kiss on to her upturned mouth. 'And do you know something, Danger Girl? I wouldn't have it any other way!'

The Beginning!

You can buy any of these other
Little Black Dress titles from your
bookshop or *direct from the publisher*.

FREE P&P AND UK DELIVERY
(Overseas and Ireland £3.50 per book)

Nina Jones and the Temple of Gloom	Julie Cohen	£5.99
Improper Relations	Janet Mullany	£5.99
Bittersweet	Sarah Monk	£5.99
The Death of Bridezilla	Laurie Brown	£5.99
Crystal Clear	Nell Dixon	£5.99
Talk of the Town	Suzanne Macpherson	£5.99
A Date in Your Diary	Jules Stanbridge	£5.99
The Hen Night Prophecies: Eastern Promise	Jessica Fox	£5.99
The Hen Night Prophecies: The One that Got Away	Jessica Fox	£5.99
The Hen Night Prophecies: Hard to Get	Jessica Fox	£5.99
A Romantic Getaway	Sarah Monk	£5.99
Trick or Treat	Sally Anne Morris	£5.99
Blue Remembered Heels	Nell Dixon	£5.99
Handbags and Homicide	Dorothy Howell	£5.99
Heartless	Alison Gaylin	£5.99
Animal Instincts	Nell Dixon	£5.99
A Most Lamentable Comedy	Janet Mullany	£5.99
Shoulder Bags and Shootings	Dorothy Howell	£5.99
Perfect Image	Marisa Heath	£5.99
Girl From Mars	Julie Cohen	£5.99

TO ORDER SIMPLY CALL THIS NUMBER

01235 400 414

or visit our website: www.headline.co.uk

Prices and availability subject to change without notice.